stories in the minor key
M. Regan

Sobelo Books

Book Cover by Drew Huff

Edited by L.C. Marino and L.P. Hernandez

ISBN (paperback): 978-1-965389-26-3
ISBN (ebook): 978-1-965389-25-6

First edition 2025

Contents

“Du bist mein und ich bin dein, und kein Men-
sch auf der Welt kann das ändern.”
— The Brothers Grimm

i. deep

The darkness pulses.

Like the heart of some ancient beast, the darkness pulses. Cold. The crush of it threatens her bones, each push-pull contraction keeping her captive within that cavern.

The heart beats. It beats against her, full of life. Draining life. Sweetwater, effervescent with oxygen, sluices from her mouth in torrents, only to flow backwards into that same chasm. The flux of fluids is grinding her teeth into pebbles.

There is a beach made of similar stones some way in the distance, but she can no longer say which direction. The hiss of the sea on the shore has been muffled by a rushing in her ears. Her thoughts are rushing, too.

Other things begin to slow.

Her own heart, smaller and finished with raging, now shudders in the aftershocks of the waters. Impassioned waves slap at the lake's surface; a tantrum of white-capped hands caress, hold, *push* her down.

Deeper. Deeper.

Bubbles weave silvery shackles through her fingers, binding her wrists and tangling her legs. She cannot fight them off. She cannot fight. She hangs in dark suspension, held by an illusionary weightlessness. She *sinks*, drawn into oblivion with the serenity of the summoned. Her eyes are wide, but she sees nothing.

She sees everything.

She sees—

The ceiling, its tiles the color of Superior's sprays. For an instant, visions and realities mingle behind bulging eyes; her stomach drops like a rock, terror rippling through her body. Bedsprings squeak, their tinny squeal grating. Clarity returns to find her prone atop her mattress, limbs tense and chest tight.

Deep breaths. Take a deep breath.

She tries. Sweat spills down her brow in streaming varicose patterns, dewing beneath the fabric of her sweatshirt and leaving her sopping wet. If not for the sheets snarled around her, she probably would have fallen out of bed.

She feels as if she had anyway. She feels winded. A metallic taste has soured her mouth, her tongue shriveling away from the backs of her teeth. Once silent, the calm of the moonlit bedroom is shattered by fish-gasps.

Take a deep breath.

Slowly, *slowly*, she is able to follow her own command, a slug of saliva smothering what tingles in her throat. The body cannot stay on high alert for long, she knows; one cannot be engulfed by anxiety if they are forced to breathe deep. That much is a scientific fact. It has been tested and proven.

After this past year, she knows how to coerce her body to calmness.

The clock on the nightstand glows an eerie green, not unlike those clocks in the B-rated horror flicks her father liked. The thought is grounding. It stands to follow, because she is on the ground. Or on land, anyway.

She is on land.

Of course she is on land. Her final wheeze snares on a snort, stifled by the hand that she draws over her face. She hadn't really wanted to see the time, but it is too late now.

She had looked. She knows.

It seems like a waste not to do anything with that knowledge, so she untangles herself from the sailors' knots of her bedding and swipes at the crumpled carton of cigarettes that lies on the nightstand. They feel soggy, but usable. Conveniently, she had forgotten to take her lighter out of her pocket. Its heft tugs against the loose material of her sleep pants, pulling the waist-band over the jut of her hip. She wears her pajamas as crookedly as she does her frown.

"Dammit," she mumbles, because it feels like the sort of thing a person should mumble after whatever-it-was she just endured. A night terror? It had been too vivid to be an ordinary dream. She curses again, because it is better than crying. "God *dammit.*"

Beyond the window, the lake berates her crassness. The frigid surf sighs its disapproval against the shore, one reedy whisper surmounted by another, then another, then another, until a chorus of condemnation censors the scuffle of her feet over moist carpet. A particularly emphatic undulation suppresses a grunt of disgust, as well.

Her hair is one capsized freighter away from being an oil spill. The slimy strands leave a line of drip-drops behind her, trailing from the bed to the door in the fashion of fairytale breadcrumbs. She is reminded of the breadcrumbs she used to feed the gulls when she visited Grand Marais. How the birds would chase her along the shore out of hope and greediness.

The thought is peculiarly poignant. Drip-drops, breadcrumbs. Tossing scraps to whatever lived near the coasts of Superior. She thinks of the scavengers that had followed her, and what else might have done the same, given half the chance.

Another breath rattles down her throat. But as the details of her nightmare ebb away, so too does the nervous energy required to experience paranoia. She has lost the power to panic. It is a welcome change.

It is odd.

But she is calm. The throbbing in her chest is receding, replaced by a detached serenity and the vague sensation of floating. Her mind is sent adrift, like lost sandals in the water.

It is a bizarre analogy, she acknowledges. That it feels significant is probably of no consequence, given the time of night. Many foolish things feel profound in the wee hours, just as many mundane things become disturbing. Thinking on it, this phenomenon is probably to blame for her having bad dreams in the first place; her reading that morning had not been especially savory.

Unlatching the door to the porch and pushing through, she reflects on her research as light reflects off the sea.

Drowning. She couldn't resist another Google search. In the weeks following her parents' funeral, she had done many Google searches, and every account featured survivors claiming that drowning isn't a bad way to go. That the initial agony of having one's life literally extinguished melts into a sort of dreamy tranquility as the brain starves for oxygen; when a person's grasp on consciousness becomes tenuous, their ability to process pain decreases. After a certain point, it is like falling asleep.

There had been relief in learning that. Or something close enough to relief for her to willfully misinterpret it. Either way, it is nice to imagine that her parents hadn't suffered as much as they could have. Her mother's corpse had borne abuse from the wreck, yes, and half of her father had never been found—torn in two by the tide, she remembers someone telling her—but the physical act of drowning would have been relatively peaceful, in the great scheme of things.

The silver lining of her thoughts materializes as she pads onto the patio, embodied in the argent halo that has formed around the moon. Smelted rays of light dribble onto the surface of Superior, congealing into glimmering scales. She makes a seat for herself on the three narrow steps that lead to the yard, tapping a cigarette from its carton and pulling the lighter from her pocket. There is the click of striking metal, the sizzle of ignition.

She tosses both carton and lighter away and admires the tip of the cigarette, blazing rosy gold. It mocks the pinprick call of a lighthouse. Of the sun that is hours from dawning.

If only this parody would imbue the latter's warmth. She is freezing. A smart person would have chosen a shower over nicotine, but she has never considered herself to be exceptionally smart.

Besides, now that she's here, there is no point going back.

Wearily, she watches the starry end of her cigarette as it rises and sets, orbiting purposefully between her lips and her knee. It feels like weeks are going by, days and nights sent spinning out of control. A year of madness.

"Take a deep breath," she reminds herself, her boyfriend's sage advice the first thing to pop into her head during these moments of stress. "Take a deep breath."

"Erin...?"

Speak of the devil.

Given the hour and the darkness and her presumed solitude, Erin thinks Mannie's voice should startle her. It does not. Somehow, she had expected him. Maybe she had even been waiting for him. He had a way of finding her during times of trouble; perhaps the real surprise is that he had not appeared earlier.

She wonders the reason for his delay.

"Erin?"

Mannie clutches to the side of Erin's little house, as gangly in the gloom as a detached silhouette. Though well into his twenties, his proportions grant him the youthful look of a high schooler, his cobbled physique that of a boy held in puberty's clutches.

One lanky arm is braced against aluminum siding. The other swings like a pendulum, its momentum helping to propel Mannie forward on buckling legs.

One foot, then the other. Then the first catches his stumble. It is unnerving to see him moving like this. Erin is not sure if she can even call it *moving*. It is more like watching a very slow fall, his body top-heavy and toppling. Though Mannie has never been graceful, he toddles now with the gait of a drunken sailor, forced to cling to the wall and its promise of balance.

He wavers, his limbs disobedient.

He watches her, just as she watches him.

A palm drags along aluminum with a yawning screech.

"Erin," Mannie says a third time, sounding pleased to see her. A smile complements the greeting, his lips pulled back to reveal a mouthful of those same silvery scales that crest the lake. The moon does strange things to water and those who live around it. "How are you feeling?"

Erin grunts. The noise is punctuated by another drag from her cigarette. She is dismissive, inhaling, allowing smoke to fill her lungs as seawater would. The singe of it smolders within her ribs for as long as she dares to hold her breath, which is not as long as she would have liked. Twenty-six seconds, and she is expelling a series of hazy rings. Lifesavers, she thinks wryly.

The burn goes away when she breathes in.

He is moving again. Not moving. Moonlight seeps around his curves, its incandescent strings animating the shadow puppet he has cast over the yard. Each step elongates his outline into something inhumanly lean, his legs disproportionately short compared to the trunk of his body.

"Not well?" her boyfriend guesses. The question is underscored by the squeal of warped paneling. He is edging closer. Closer. Doused in eventide, his hand is the color of wet sand against the wall. He cleaves to the siding with gritty tenacity. "You look like you saw a ghost. Or something worse, maybe. Like a monster."

Though summer, the night is crisp. If Erin is uncomfortable in her moist pajamas, then Mannie must be miserable. His clothes are thin. They cling to his body in translucent patches, swatches of fabric stuck to his flesh and framed by pale folds. Distantly, Erin wonders if he had been victimized by nightmares, too. It would be quite the coincidence, if so. Still she feels like it is possible.

She feels like she is forgetting something.

"Erin? Cryptid got your tongue?"

A thin cloud wanders before the moon. Her cigarette threatens to blister her knuckles.

"Sorry, sorry. Thinking," she mutters, flicking the stub onto the bottom step. Her feet are bare, but that does not stop her from stamping the butt into a shining streak, like kids do when killing fireflies. Its glow fades. The world is blacker than ever.

"Thinking? What about?"

Death, is the answer she should give.

"A bad dream" is the answer she does give. "I had one. As an anniversary present, I bet."

"Ahhh." Mannie hums, his tone pitching up, then down. There is a lilt to it that he seems to hope will soothe. "Well. It *has* been a full year."

"It has."

"Then unless you really *did* see a monster, that explains it."

"It explains *something*," Erin agrees. Disagrees. She scrutinizes the arc of ash before her, the ball of her foot tingling where it was intimate with embers. It doesn't hurt as much as she assumed it would. It doesn't really hurt at all. Pressing her foot flat to the step, Erin thinks back to more dire injuries, like the time she stepped on a glass shard.

Mannie had been with her then, too. He had been the one to see her fall, to hear her scream. He had been the first to lope across the beach to her rescue, bounding along the shore like a lifeguard in an old episode of Baywatch. Literally, given that he could only run as fast as a slow-motion David Hasselhoff.

It was a touching response. She was too distracted to appreciate that at the time, but in retrospect she loves him for it. Her boyfriend, face shining bronze in the sun, made for quite a sight as he leapt over driftwood and trash to rescue her from almost-certain tetanus.

In the hospital, Mannie had been equally attentive. A shared fondness for grim humor had him joking that both of their feet would need to be amputated, but at least they could take solace in being gimps together.

He was teasing. Of course he was. Still, Erin remembers pushing for Mannie to get looked at, too. The same weak legs that kept him from sprinting also served as a warning against heavy lifting, yet he insisted on carrying her into the ER. If he hurt himself in the process...

The suggestion was waved off. He was fine, Mannie assured, and his legs were unimportant in the long run. What *was* important was staying with her. He was adamant that he stay with her.

He stayed with her. He was there through an injection and three stitches, and has ever since insisted that she wear boots like him. Or sandals, at least.

Erin curls her toes inward. She curls them out, wondering where those sandals are. She put on her favorite pair before leaving for the beach that afternoon, and always returned them to the basket beside the door after coming home.

She doesn't remember seeing them tonight. Where are they? She never takes them off outside, so she couldn't have forgotten them.

Could she?

Had she?

She is forgetting something, something important. The realization slithers lazily in the pit of her belly, winding through the coils of her intestines. It niggles in the back of her brain, asking for her attention.

It is not alone in wanting it.

The quiet. It is too quiet, she notices. Conspicuously so. There is no familiar *clump-clap* of rubber soles, no flint-and-tinder strike of lace caps against stud hooks. Instead of rhythmic clomping, there is only the protest of disturbed gravel. Pebbles chitter against one another as they are kicked, tattle-telling on the beach that is constantly trying to sneak its way into her home. Past the jagged pickets of a rambling fence, down the slope of a rocky incline, the lake laps at a bank that seems determined to make Erin's yard a part of itself.

It gains inches. So does Mannie.

Why isn't he wearing his boots? That isn't like him at all. Mannie always wears his boots. Even inside, because of his weak ankles. She wants to ask but isn't sure how to do that without sounding deranged. It would be a weird thing to interrogate him about.

Besides, they are already having a conversation.

"It only explains *something*? Is there a different answer that you're looking for?" Mannie wonders, in a voice barely louder than his shuffling feet. The similarly shuffling waters wave goodbye to the moon as a roving plume of nothingness engulfs it.

Erin's hair weeps at the loss. The disheveled strands sob over the patio, splattering against the lathwork in a harmonizing refrain of soprano *plips*. Stains become deep puddles.

She considers lighting another cigarette, if only for the meager glow it would provide. Those puddles behind her are the color of spilled ink. The lake before her is a void. To step off the coast would be like stepping off the edge of the world, then falling into something deeper than space. Ebony veils blot out the stars above, the diaphanous palls susurrating one atop the other, undulant. Static forms between their layers, illuminating the clouds' underbellies with the first flickering hints of lightning.

Red skies in the morning, sailors take warning, her father always said. Erin doesn't remember red skies this morning. She feels like she mentioned as much to Mannie when he dragged her to the docks that afternoon. *Red skies at night, sailors' delight.*

"What are you looking for, Erin?"

What might delight when the sky isn't red?

Erin frowns.

"Not a different *answer*. Not necessarily. Just... something *else*," she confesses, nose scrunching. But composure remains, much as the pocket pools that Superior leaves in the rocks during low tide. Even without the moon, high tide returns; there is a bubbling in her brain as thoughts well up, rushing to fill her head with the memories that sleep earlier washed away. Erin may have forgotten something, but she feels on the cusp of grasping it again.

Wading towards that lost knowledge, she speculates, "Maybe what I'm looking for is an actual *thing*."

"What kind of thing?"

"I don't know. If I knew, I wouldn't be looking," she sighs. She thinks she might normally sound petulant when answering such a question, but right now she is too distracted to muster the energy for sarcasm.

She is close. So close. What is she forgetting? Her mind gurgles, a frosty sensation draining down her spine. Or maybe that's her hair. She licks her lips, though they are already wet.

"Do you remember me telling you," Erin murmurs, "that when I was a kid, I read a book about monsters in the lake? Like, sea serpents and stuff? I used to go down to Artists' Point and sit on the rocks and wait to see one."

It was an old habit, monster-watching. Not a bad one, not like the smoking, but something else she overindulged in. Or she used to, anyway. The past year changed that, like it had so much else. Nowadays, she has a cigarette in her hands more often than her binoculars. She spends more time on search engines than on searching. And while Erin does not avoid the lake exactly, neither does she pine for its mysteries like when she was little.

And yet, nostalgia is as powerful as any undertow. It pulls her back at the most unexpected times. She remembers with poignant intensity the anticipation that drove her younger self: the rising heartbeats and falling stomachs that accompanied every misshapen piece of driftwood she spotted. She would stare out over eternity and feel so certain that she would someday see *something*, because it was only fair. It was only a matter of time. She could be patient.

Standing amidst the stacked stones that tourists left as tribute to the waters, she would hold her breath and think, just one more minute. Just one more. One more.

There had to be something there.

There has to be.

There is.

It is a belief that Erin holds to like others hold to God. It is her own private faith.

Or it had been private, anyway.

That changed earlier today, when she told all this to Mannie. Nerves made her chatty while helping him cast his tiny ship, and she was even worse when made to actually sit in it. Bobbling atop the surf, Erin decided the perceived threat of the supernatural gave warped credence to the terror she felt when staring into the blue-black depths.

It was hardly logical. She knew that. Knows that. But beliefs are rarely based on logic, and for some reason, when called upon to face her true fears, it felt less childish to say that she still believes in monsters.

A few yards out, and it was impossible to see Superior's bottom. A few miles, and even the shore vanished. Erin read once that scientists know more about the cosmos than they do about the sea, and she can understand why: there is a hint of the divine in the desire to look up. Everyone knows that's where Heaven is.

They also know what waits down below.

She knew what waited down below.

A necropolis lurked beneath their craft, its gravestones made of rusted iron and broken planks and entombed skeletons. To remember as much awakened in Erin a sickening sort of clarity; she mulled on her own life's transience while imagining the remains of sunken schooners and cargo liners. Her parents' dinghy. They were testaments to the frailty of human existence. They were more than she could bear.

Better to talk of giant squids or Pressie.

Mannie, then understanding, responded with a laugh, wondering aloud how much money they would make if they caught and stuffed Mishibizhiw.

Mannie, now curious, has one hand around the porch's railing and both eyes upon Erin.

"So did you? Ever see one, I mean," he asks, hefting himself to the steps with the help of the banisters.

His legs are trembling beneath him, jerking like a dying thing. Shivers, she assumes. Dark liquid is scattered in splotches behind him, and Erin reflects again on breadcrumbs. Things that lead and those that follow.

She allows him to lead the conversation, following its flow even though the question was an odd one. Hadn't they talked about this earlier? He should know the answer.

"Yes," Erin tells him without hesitation.

Wait.

She falters, confused. Her mind catches up with her mouth.

"No," Erin tries again, speaking more carefully this time. The word contorts her features into a series of unpleasant shapes, finishing with a grimace.

That tasted like a lie, but it wasn't. She had never seen anything. Not anything more fanciful than July's dragon boats, anyway. And a few crazy swimmers. And some gulls.

With mounting curiosity, Erin ponders her first reaction. She spoke so bluntly, so decisively. Never mind what Mannie knows—does *she* know the truth? What happened?

What is she forgetting?

This would be very worrisome if she could bring herself to worry.

It is late. She is tired. All the same, Erin makes a token effort to demonstrate bemusement, because she feels like she should. She kneads at her forehead, listening to her thoughts slosh between her ears.

Water sloshes against the shore.

Waves had sloshed against their boat as well, the vessel's pendulum sway enough to hypnotize. She had stared mindlessly over the glass of the surface, searching for interesting reflections as Mannie prepared a fishing rod.

"…I liked the stories," Erin mumbles, lifting her eyes to stare dreamily over those same waters. The blackness of the sky reflects the blackness of the lake, their blend seamless.

A storm is brewing. That which had been two is now one is now calamity, and the edge of the world has become the end of it. She does not fear impending dangers.

She is calm. Placid. Like the meadowsweet blossoms that sometimes tumble into the lake, only to be dragged limply, unresisting, into its fathoms.

She says, "I've *always* liked the stories. I've always liked to imagine that the world isn't really so boring. That there's a little magic in it. But after this year…

"After this year, I wanted something to blame, you know? I wanted something to hate and be angry at. Some people decide to be angry at God, but I've never really felt His presence. Not in the same way I feel Superior's. So if I was going to blame something…"

She is forgetting something.

"Well, here's something."

Mannie has lowered himself atop the tiered steps, his feet grotesquely pigeon-toed. They are streaked with mud, she notices. Thick, and moist, and starting to crust. He really had lost his boots. A while ago, apparently. With effort, Mannie scoots himself closer to Erin, his dank shoulder knocking against her own as if trying to imbue some sense. Some*thing*.

There is something missing, something that should be here but isn't. Something she should have noticed earlier, when she had been sprawled and soaked atop her bed. It all connects to the something she has forgotten. It *is* the something she has forgotten.

"In 1782," Mannie begins, gazing out over the churning lake, "a man named Venant St. Germain and a few of his fellows were scouting the land near Thunder Bay. They were helped by an Ojibwe guide. Sometime into their mission, the voyagers spotted a figure offshore—a being with the head and the torso of a human. Venant later gave testimony in court, swearing that the creature had been a boy-child from the waist up, with a handsome head and brilliant eyes. A merman, he claimed.

"As is the way of white invaders, one of his companions moved to shoot the merman. However, their guide stopped him. Petrified, she referred to the being as Maymaygwashi, the God of Lakes and Waters. At her insistence, the group moved far from Gitchi-Gami, seeking higher ground. She said a storm would no doubt be coming to punish those who had laid their eyes upon a god.

"The voyagers thought that the woman was superstitious, of course, but they followed her instructions. And it was lucky for them that they did, for that very same evening saw a terrible tempest strike the Bay and ravage the area for days."

As he speaks, Erin listens, thoughts converging. There is a familiarity to the tale, a sort of déjà vu that she cannot quite place. The chill of it rises up the back of her throat, burbling like bile. Or water.

The body is 60% water, she learned in school. Everyone is a lake in and of themselves. Or an ocean, maybe. Sweat is famously brackish.

Brackish.

And there it is. *There it is.* The thing that she had been missing. Erin's eyes widen, her body liquefying all the further when she finally makes the connection.

There is no salt.

She is soaked, and he is soaked, and there is not a drop of salt between them. They are drenched, but not in sweat. She thought it was sweat. It cannot be sweat. She does not smell salt.

She does not smell anything.

She does not remember leaving the lake.

Mannie smiles again, and Erin shouldn't be able to see the vivid blue of his irises through the gloom, but she can.

"I'm glad I could finally tell you that. It makes me happy to give you what you want. I always want to give you what you want," he says shyly, placing a broad hand atop her knee. Tacky fluids stain the material where his fingers fall. The touch does not feel as warm as it should. Erin wonders why. She wonders why she isn't frightened.

Her arms are leaden where they lay, but her heart is less weighted. The organ bobs, up and down like a boat on glossy waters. Like a tiny ship against a mounting eagre.

"And how exactly is that 'what I want?'" Erin contests, exhaling the words on a shallow breath. She feels it rushing through her teeth, tumbling, spilling. "Are you telling me that this Maymaygwashi thing exists? That it killed my parents?"

Mannie chuckles again. It is a sad sound, accompanied by a sympathetic pat.

The night has become so murky that it takes his leaning over for Erin to realize that her field of vision has narrowed. A nebulous haze traces the contours of Mannie's face, framing an expression of empathy.

"Not your mother," he whispers.

Erin's feet feel very cold. Thunder cracks. Sonic reverberations rend splinters into the mirror of the lake and the edifice of the clouds, the broken reflections of sky and sea shrieking in protest when shards of rain grind free. Frozen droplets shatter against Erin's shoulders as piercing as glass.

Already familiar with such pain, she does not notice their bite.

"Your mother was dead when Maymaygwashi found her, her eyes like milk and mouth open like a fish," Mannie persists, pushing a tendril of hair behind Erin's ear. The forelock cleaves to her temple in seaweed snarls, its auburn hue strangely virescent in the eddying dim. The maelstrom has granted everything a green-gray tint, Erin notices, Mannie's gaze included. It swims before her as he adds, "But your father was a fighter, like the fur trappers from whom he was descended. Like you. He reminded the merman of you. The awe and the terror on his face was the same as the awe and the terror so often on yours, back when you would spend hours and hours on the rocks at Artists' Point. It was the same awe and terror that you rediscovered today, floundering as you were pulled under by a riptide."

The tempest around them intensifies, the distant whine of its winds blustering into a howl. Trees bend and bow, kowtowing to Superior forces. Angry gusts shove against Erin's back, urging her to show the same respect. She resists, though through no great display of stubbornness. She simply cannot move forward. Mannie has angled himself around her with tender purpose, his hands on her cheeks and his knees bracing hers.

His wrists, thin and elegant, are perfect, unblemished, and dark. They are the stark opposite of her wrists. Of her bare feet. Of his own feet, glanced beneath the fringe of her lashes.

The storm has cleaned away layers of grime, revealing skin that is imperfect, blemished, and white.

"I hadn't intended to do this so soon. Someday, yes. I would have to *someday*, given your ancestry. But not today. I really *was* happy just to be with you," he apologizes, in a muted tenor that carries effortlessly over the wailing of the squall. "But when you agreed to come out with me, I couldn't help it. I have missed Gitchi-Gami more than I can say. The lake is sacred, you know. I *know* you know. You can feel it, too. Your fear is a healthy part of that respect, and I appreciate it. But still, I hated to see you avoid the waters. I wanted you to admire the lake's beauty again. Your childhood admiration of the lake was one of the things I first found so attractive about you. It was why I took the time to know you.

"I wouldn't have let that swell hurt you," Mannie continues, flashing Erin a boyish pout. "But you panicked. You grabbed me, and for as much sway as I have over the lake, I have none over boats. Boats are from land. I couldn't stop us from overturning. I am sorry about that. And about what happened next."

What happened next? Next had been darkness. And in that darkness, she had seen—

"To mix the magicks of earth and the magicks of water is to turn both into mud. The spell that I cast on these legs melted away, and I cannot use them twice for the same purpose. Not effectively."

Mannie's palms are clammy, his voice cool and collected. Erin feels her body relax further into his embrace, even as her brain muzzily suggests that she panic.

What he is saying makes no sense. It makes a lot of sense. It makes sense in that way that dreams do when having them, but upon waking all semblance of reason dribbles away like water through cupped hands. And there is so much water here. It cascades around them in gallons, pushing down on their shoulders and spines. Never has there been a heavier rain. She watches, languidly composed, as the weight of it proves too much for Mannie's right leg.

There is a snap of sinew. His thigh caves to pressure with the nonchalance of a doll's, sagging away from his lower hip. His ankle rolls. Detached, the pale limb wobbles, the tight sheath of his jeans the only thing keeping it from breaking away entirely.

"Your leg fell off," Erin points out, as if he may have missed this. Mannie chortles, affectionate.

"It wasn't really mine to start with."

Oh.

"Are you going to take my legs?" Erin asks, with more misty curiosity than concern. The deluge drapes over the pair in thick sheets, blanketing them from the rest of the world.

For the first time, Mannie looks taken aback. Mortified, even.

"No, I'm not. I would never do that to you."

"Are you going to kill me, then?"

"You are already dead."

The ice in Erin's extremities has traveled inward, leaving a slushy sensation between her fingers and toes. It tingles, but it also numbs. It is a feeling that saps away all others, and she is left as vaguely aware of her own body as she is the reality that the rain is washing away.

The world floods. There is only Mannie now, keeping her anchored to this place. To this moment.

"You are drowning, Erin," Mannie gently clarifies, his voice echoing over the thrum of the tempest. There is a roaring in her ears she thought was blood. Maybe not. "As we speak, you and I are in my lake. This is happening in your mind, with as much realism as I can muster. You are blacking out, though.

The electricity in your synapses is short-circuiting. It looks like lightning. I am smothering it. You are filling with my waters. I am inside your lungs and your head. I am replacing the oxygen in your blood, controlling it as I control what rages above and below us."

Erin ruminates on this, oozing a sleepy sound of understanding. She should be afraid, but she cannot find the energy.

Her limbs are useless. Her hair is peeling from her nape, feathering behind her as the rainfall becomes an unbroken torrent, and that torrent fully congeals.

"If you can do so much," she slurs, the words streaming from her in a chain, "why aren't you saving me?"

Mannie cocks his head, bemused. The details of his expression have begun to bleed together, blurred by her rippling vision. Everything is glazing over. All she can see now are his eyes, glimmering with the opalescence of abalone.

"Because you saw me."

Ah. That's right. The story. She supposes that's the reason he told it in the first place, to avoid having to answer such stupid questions. Erin thinks she might be embarrassed about having failed to live up to his expectations, but what is the point if she isn't going to live? The sentiment soon passes. Everything does, her mind dissolving into sea foam.

Thoughts fizzle through her nostrils, escaping her in wisps. The lake has a way of making sharp things dull, rounding their edges and wearing them smooth. Glass, stone, the human consciousness.

Submerged and sinking, Erin can already feel herself eroding, reduced to a shell of what she had been.

"I don't want to die like my parents," she mouths, the confession pulled from her throat by the hands of the tide. It flows between her lips, unfettered by stirrings of urgency or dread. It is simply the truth. Propelled by bubbles, the admission is soon lost to the current, swept out to sea along with her sense of self. It slips away like sandals, gifted to Superior.

Mannie simpers, not unkindly.

"You won't," he assures. There are fingers around Erin's neck, the appendages long and thin. Spidery. Webbed? She cannot see their splay, but the pressure paralyzing her is enough to make one thing very clear.

He is holding her in place. He is holding her down. He is tightening his grip, and as he does so, he is promising, "You won't die like them, from a blow to the head or evisceration. I want you to have what you want, because I love you, Erin. I always have, since the day I first saw you on the rocks, sharing your bread with the gulls. I saw you, and now—now, you have seen me, too. Now, your soul will join me in the waters. Are you ready?"

She does not respond. The light in her eyes is flickering like the embers of a cigarette.

"Take a deep breath," the god advises.

The light winks out.

Major Key Inspirations:
The Little Mermaid
and Lore of the Great Lakes

ii. holy water

"I read somewhere that there's no such thing as 'new wa ter.'"

My response to this—a prompting, lilted hum—resounds against the warped sides of my portable bathtub, echoing within the dents that years and negligence have carved into tin curves. You have dropped it more than once during our travels. Last week, when you tripped in the wastes of yet another nameless, desiccated city, the tub was nearly ruined by debris. Nearly punctured by the scattered incisors made by ruined window-panes.

Nearly. But it wasn't. Instead, the tin's cacophonous clatter resounded down the streets, redolent of an overdue death knell. So that was all right. If we have learned anything during our travels, it is that a tub like this can withstand a fair amount of clumsiness. It is not as fragile as the conch shell, or the jars, or the sea glass mobile that you are presently struggling to untangle.

"I don't remember where, anymore. Where I read it, I mean."

There is sweat on your brow. Your upper lip. Under your arms. From the heat, I suspect. But your fingers remain pale, despite the weather's endless efforts. I watch them as they twitch:

sleek and silvery minnows, wriggling on the ends of varicose lines.

Your veins are so beautifully blue. Your wrists are so stunningly scarred.

You are, as ever, so exquisitely human.

"Give that to me, my dear," I gently command, reaching out with hands that are *not*. Not pale, not scarred. Not *human*. Once upon a time, these hands wove *jiāo xiāo shā* silk with incomparable ease.

That was lives ago, of course. Bodies ago.

But water remembers.

There is gratitude in your grin when you pass me the snarled sun catcher, its kaleidoscopic shards dripping down my arms with the clarity of dew, the chill of a fresh spray. Light spills off my elbows and onto the moldy tile floor, shifting and swimming and silent. Ephemeral flotsam.

"Don't get me wrong, I know it could have been, like... one of those pseudo-science articles?" you continue. There is a tidal predictability to your attention; as I watch, your gaze flows over to the jars. What remains in them is mostly condensation, at this point: the brine pooled in their bottoms shallow enough to look accidental. Which it is, in a way. Certainly we did not intend for their levels to get so low. But it also isn't, because what could we do? I try not to hear the weariness in your sigh, focused instead on the melancholic tinkle of the glass I am unwinding. "You know, those articles that use just enough logic and primary school science to make a claim that sounds plausible, and then everyone just... just *believes* it, because those half-lies are easier to wrap your head around than the overly complicated truth of the matter?"

"Mmm," I hum again. In the deep, private darkness of my own mind, I recall my brief existence as *Amabie*, scaly and bird-billed, and the day that I met another you-before-you on a beach in Higo Province. The Land of the Rising Sun was like another world entirely beneath twilight's purple shroud, and the shoreline echoed with the demand for which that time of day was colloquially named.

Tasokare—who are you?

It was a good question then. It is a good question now. In answer, I allowed my oracular aura to pulse and expand, to illume that liminal space between sand and sea, day and night, natural and preternatural.

For six more years, the harvests will be bountiful, I deigned to inform that version of you. *Should illness strike, show the suffering my picture to cure them.*

Everything came to pass exactly as I predicted, and there was no science involved at all, pseudo or otherwise. What might *this* iteration say about that revelation, if you remembered?

You may yet remember, someday.

Water remembers.

"The way this article phrased it," you tell me, working to uncork those hollow, hallowed jars, "is that Earth started with a certain amount of water. In glaciers, in the ocean. In lakes and rivers or whatever. 71% of the planet's total surface, trapped here by our atmosphere."

"Right."

"And that same amount has been caught in the hydrologic cycle since then," you grunt, one cork giving you particular trouble. Wound braids of rope chafe against your jeans when you brace the knot-ornamented bottle between your thighs, clearly hoping better leverage will help you wiggle the stopper free from its salt-crusted neck. When it does not, you set the whole of it aside to deal with later, rather than accidentally shatter something in frustration. "So basically, any cup of water I might pour for myself will have already gone through the system of a dinosaur, and Socrates, and Mary Magdalene and, I dunno, Jacques Cousteau."

"From what I understand, Jacques Cousteau did interact with quite a bit of water before he died," I comment in tones made mild by humor. The mobile hangs freely now, its bobbles and beads twirling on their weedy threads. I delight in this pretty pleasure, recalling with fondness those similar strings that were plaited into the hair of my kelpie body. There are still days when I miss the lochs of Ross and Cromarty—the teeth-sharp ridges and damp-gray gullets of the Scottish Highlands—but I was really only there for you.

Besides, the lochs are probably gone. Most lakes are. Most rivers, too.

Will there be any ocean left, I wonder, by the time we find the coast?

"Hey." You smile, a comforting thing. And I am comforted, though perhaps not for the reasons you assume. "I'm sorry. Don't worry about it, all right? It probably wasn't an accurate article."

Compassion further curls the corners of your lips. Lopsided, the expression crests like a wave: rising, falling. Crashing. In its wake, sentiment sweeps over me, followed by a warm wash of affection, and I barely resist the urge to drag you down, to pull you under, when you lean forward to collect the sun catcher.

I would have dragged you down, once. I *did* pull you under, once. Eons have passed since then, but you have still never been more gorgeous than you were the day you drowned in my embrace, your throat strung with silver bubbles and the whites of your eyes nacre-bright.

"Now that we're talking about it, I'm pretty sure I read somewhere *else* that the Earth is always creating new water. In its crust and stuff. Although, well, it's obviously not producing it fast enough."

"Not its fault, really," I murmur, turning in the tub's basin. The perpetually wet fabric of my nixie skirt sticks to metal walls, and I bunch the soggy sheaves more comfortably around my legs before adding, "If that is so, I mean. There is a lot to keep up with, here on the surface. Thirsty animals, greedy people. Storms and heat that nothing was meant to survive. Not everyone was trained to treat precious resources with the respect and care that you were, Amaya."

My praise adds an undercurrent of pride to your beam. The mobile is lain across a tattered grimoire, gingerly arranged so that its components cannot retwist themselves before you have a chance to hang it beside the grit-scabbed casement of the hovel that we are squatting in for the night.

Once that is taken care of, you reach out again, offering me your hands.

"Water is sacred," you whisper. I nod, slipping my fingers between your own with all the reverence you deserve.

"Your body is my temple," I breathe in reply. And it is, *it is*. A shrine unto me, recycled and reprocessed, built and rebuilt over ceaseless centuries. What magic you now possess has been condensed from that which was contained in the yous-before-you, each of your previous incarnations strong enough to hold me in their cupped palms for a little longer, a little longer. Drop by drop by drop by drop, you have amassed holier fractions, more consecrated ratios. You have stored them in the sodden vessel of your brain, your heart. Your lungs, your kidneys, your blood, your skin. Even your bones are 31% brackish and blessed.

For now.

For now.

But there is more to us than *now*, even if you do not remember. Even if you never remember, though I suspect you will. Eventually. Water does not just have memory: it has patience. It is impossibly, inhumanly patient. And though I have not told you yet, I already know how our story will end.

When layers dissolve and tissues return to dust—

When the rains stop forever, and the desert overtakes the sea—

When the last tenacious puddle has dispersed into the ether, and all life has been compressed into a single, pearly tear—

You and I will be one, my love. You and I will be complete.

"Undine," you murmur, urging our joined hands towards my fangs. Your wrist is softer than sponge in my mouth. My tongue is sharp enough to gouge new scars. "Undine, help me worship you."

Obliging, devoted, my teeth sink down.
And together, we fill my tub.

Major Key Inspirations:
Legends of Jiāorén, Amabie,
Kelpie, Nixie, and Undine

iii. sparrow

*I. ("Who killed Cock Robin?" "I," said the Sparrow,
"With my bow and arrow, I killed Cock Robin.")*

———◦———

II. I am alive.

I live in the corners, dusty and dark. I hide behind furnishings, frightened by sunlight. I chase after his shadow, and I pounce on his heels.

His shadow is my favorite place to be. I love it there. I feel safe in the shape of him, warm and surrounded, as if we were embracing. My fingers dig playfully into his ankles, into the tendons and skin and brittle bones that have been cloistered inside his boots.

He cannot see me. He cannot feel me. But a shiver races up his spine, and he knows that I am there.

———◦———

III. Mornings are too bright for silhouettes.

In the office, bow windows shine like crystal, their lattices bleached to nihility. I crouch beside his writing desk, watching as he works.

Sometimes, I poke his inkpots. Sometimes, I rustle his mail. Sometimes, I make him smile.

Afternoon performs strange alchemy on the light, turning its watery rays thick and golden. The wash of it gilds the parlor, making baroque furnishings gleam. He takes his tea while I take my nap, lulled by the silvery song of spoons in Wedgewood cups, and when I wake, I find he has set aside a biscuit or a tiny cake for me, newspaper foregone in favor of watching cream melt and fruit glazing ooze.

I cannot eat what he eats. I cannot eat at all. But it is nice to play pretend.

Evening comes like a hundred thousand crows, their feathers smothering the sun. Plumage rustles; beady eyes gaze unnoticed from within the downy gloom. He groans and whimpers and sighs atop his feather bed, against another's body, as the moon casts delicate reflections of cage bars across the floor.

(*"Who saw him die?" "I," said the Fly,*
"With my little eye, I saw him die.")

"Is she... here...?" he asks, breathlessly wanton, his bruised lips parted and bright gaze darting. Straining, desperate, he tries to see beyond the veil that hides me from his sight.

I peek from behind the four-poster's curtain. That I am spotted immediately is a surprise to no one.

"She is, Master," the house maid chuckles, affection stitching together the tattered silk of her voice. Monochrome petticoats and pools of ruche froth around her hips. Long hair spills over bare flesh. Violet eyes cut sideways, sharp enough to slice through the atramentous night, inhuman enough to see me for what I am.

For who I am.

"...tell her to leave us."

The maid's lashes flutter, as light as a nested bird's wing.

"You heard him, little one."

A draft urges me into the hall. The corridor stretches long, so I do the same. Tendrils of my consciousness expand freely, drifting outward, and I meld peacefully into the blackness.

IV. I say nothing. I weigh nothing. I am nothing.

"No, little one. You are *everything*."

The maid's silhouette is as much a comfort to me as her Master's. I wrap around and around her legs, weaving myself through the eyelets of her boots. She pares and peels potatoes while I pout.

"Just a bit longer, dear heart. Just hold out a bit longer."

V. He sees me—metaphorically—as one would a tiny child. He sees me as innocent, as naïve and fragile.

He does not *see* me. He has never seen me, and so is far from correct in his assumptions.

But neither is he wrong.

His body is newly twenty. My essence is now two and one-half. Yet, it seems to me that we are older than we appear, our minds as wicked and ancient as the violet-eyed creature who dubbed herself his maid.

⸻ ❖ ⸻

VI. Every Christmas, I am given a doll.

They are left for me on the sill of the nursery's window, their miniature legs hooked over the crib bars. Dust motes spin as mobiles would above them. When the sun shines, its rays press warmth into china spines. I learned to tell time off the dials of dangling feet.

Hours pass. Then days, then months, then years. I change. They don't. They sit, angelified by halos of backlight, as I marvel at their beauty.

A window frame of whitewashed wood borders the brunette, the crushed velvet of her bonnet bluer than the summer sky. Beside her sits a redhead with a braid, her doe eyes wide and filamented and lifeless.

I cannot play with my dolls. I cannot move them, cannot touch them. But I can love them. I can paw at them, and sniff them, and stare. I can *want*.

I *do* want. I want a blonde this year. A blonde with curls. I want her to be pale, to wear pinks and pearls. I want this very badly. I want that want to be known.

The maid laughs when I loop myself around her skirts, begging, nearly getting lost in labyrinthine lace patterns.

"Perhaps," she coos, "if you are good."

———◆———

VII. Before there were dolls to teach me time, before there were sweets left for my pleasure, before he knew I was there at all, I saw the Master cry.

("*Who'll be chief mourner?" "I," said the Dove,*

"*I mourn for my love, I'll be chief mourner.*")

He blamed chills on the winter, jostled mail on crosswinds. His inkpot tipped due to his own carelessness, though he swore it'd been placed nowhere near his elbow.

He swore in other ways, too. Walking past me, walking through me, the Master cursed and wandered, stumbling about until he reached the manor's barren garden. He was alone there, except for the birds.

There are always, always birds.

The marble bench that the Master favors was as cold as a grave in February, as white as the snow and the sound of silence. The flowers that had been planted last spring lay withered and dead at his feet.

Branches shivered beside him, shriveled, clawing from the earth like corpse arms. They strained for him. I did, too.

Neither of us could reach.

Don't cry, I tried but could not say. I had no voice, no mouth, no face. He had no shadow in the colorless day, no idea that I was beside him, sobbing, *Please, don't be sad.*

You don't need to be sad.

I am alive.

——— ❖ ———

VIII. Sometimes, my biscuit is taken. Sometimes, my cake is eaten. Sometimes, the Lady comes to call, and decorum compels the Master to bow, gracious, and offer what would have been my share.

I do not mind. The Lady fascinates me. She is the closest one can get to sunshine without being burned, a radiant beauty comprised of golden tresses and rosy cheeks, frills and ruffles and opalescent gossamer. Pinky daintily extended, she sips at Earl Grey and flashes a smile, her teeth the exact same shade of porcelain as her cup.

Her eyes shimmer, and I can tell she loves him.

I like that, too. I touch the instep of her shoe, stroking reverentially to her heel. She does not understand that chilly static tickle, only knows that her foot suddenly, gracelessly jerks.

The Lady apologizes.

He tells her not to worry. Pours her a spot more tea. Asks her once again if she is sure, very sure, that she wishes to be his.

(*"Who'll be the parson?" "I," said the Rook, "With my little book, I'll be the parson."*)

"Yes," the Lady vows. "In every way."

He loves her, too. Obviously he loves her, too.

The wedding is in one week.

——— ❖ ———

IX. I don't like it in here.

It's dark. Hot. Wet. Too wet. What are these? I can't move. I don't recognize—I can't move. I can't breathe. I don't like it. He said I would like it. I'm trapped. I can't breathe. I can't breathe. I can'tbreathe. Icantbreathe.Icantbreatheicantbreathe*icantbreathe*—

(*"Who caught his blood?" "I," said the Fish, "With my little dish, I caught his blood."*)

A snap, a squelch. I burst into the world with a sickening *crack*, like a hatchling escaping its egg. Mist hisses, deafening. The walls are copper-damp where sprayed.

I am riled. Terrified. In a panic, I flee my prison and scramble over to their shadows, quivering as I cling to the maid's leg. She comforts me with a hush.

Then, turning to her Master, she says:

"I told you she would reject it."

⸻ ◆ ⸻

X. He had to be told.

About the vertebrae, about the viscera, about the chunks. About the slurry of half-formed organs that his maid had labored over, silent, on that starry night two and one-half years ago.

It had been an agonizing ordeal, even for one like herself. The pain overwhelmed. The horror could drive one mad. Cursing her body for its failures, the maid cried and cried, cradling what fleshy parts could be fished from the mire. She gathered a tendon, an eye, pushed through another contraction, and then, finally—

"There you were, little one."

That's what he was told, and that's what she tells me. I have to be told, too. No one really remembers being born. I don't *want* to remember being born. I coil closer to the maid, shuddering to imagine myself in so many raw lumps, splattered across ruined sheets.

"You were like a doll," the maid continues, her voice as warm as my entrails had been. "Disassembled. Broken beyond repair. But... in being what I am, I had ways to preserve your pieces."

A tender finger traces the edge of a jar, the ridge of its lid, the warped and pickled contours of what floats behind thick glass. The rate of decay is measured. The blanket nest readjusted. The stench of bitter herbs puffs up from the crib, stirring the nursery's stagnant air as dust wheels, winks, and falls like stars in the ichorous twilight.

She checks the time on my dolls. Soon, their shadows will disappear.

Soon, I will disappear.

———◆———

XI. The Master does not see me.

He cannot see me. He cannot bear to see me, not as I yet am. He stands outside the nursery door, his hand pressed flat to painted wood, and tells me I am beautiful.

He tells me that he loves me.

He tells me that he'll save me.

(*"Who'll bear the pall?" "We," said the Wren,*
"Both the cock and the hen, we'll bear the pall.")

"Leave everything to me."

XII. I like her.

The Lady is comely. She smells of gardenias. I orbit her shins, and I wonder if she would like me, too, could she see me. Would she allow me to sit on her lap and try on her jewels? Would she sing *Who Killed Cock Robin* with me, or play hide-and-go-seek?

I doubt it.

XIII. I am alive.

"Without a body, she'll have no anchor."

Living things die.

"I know."

I am dying.

"Without an anchor, she'll disappear."

I am disintegrating.

"I *know!*"

I am fading.

"There is only one choice."

Help me...

"...I know."

XIV. "Is the Lady ready to begin her new life?"

Lashes low, the maid smiles at her Master's intended: at her rouged cheeks, her glossed lips, her powdered décolletage. A veil is pinned into her ringlets, as fine as spun sugar or rime. Or cobwebs. Diamonds are stitched into its pleats, glittering like the dust to which we all return.

Blushing with excitement, the Lady beams. Behind her lay the silk of a long train, its drag reminding me of shorn wings.

"I am."

"Well," purrs the maid, "You look beautiful."

(*"Who'll make the shroud?" "I," said the Beetle,*

"With my thread and needle, I'll make the shroud.")

The praise is enough to turn the Lady's flush magenta.

But when the maid opens her preternatural eyes, the one she is looking at is me.

⸺◆⸺

XV. He enters when she leaves.

Finery suits a man as regal as the Master; he was born for gems and roses and satin. The top hat he wears is as black as his shadow, and I take an immediate shine to it.

It is beautiful. *He* is beautiful. Not her, not me. I wonder if he knows that. Does he see? Though he is gazing into the vanity's mirror, his focus is over his shoulder, not on his own reflection.

Fingertips settle upon the seatback. Cufflinks make prisms of the light. His expression is troubled, but his eyes are calm. I see them both, see *through* them both, to the soul that tarnishes behind them.

I remember the day that he cried, the day he was told. But maybe he is thinking of the day that he *believed*, for when the Master next speaks, he uses those same words he had with the maid.

("Who'll dig his grave?" "I," said the Owl,
"With my pick and shovel, I'll dig his grave.")
"Everything else be damned."

XVI. We await the bride and groom in the townhouse, away from the dangers of consecrated grounds. Being alone proves a different sort of blessing. With no Lady or servants around, the maid can openly play with me, and play she does. I hardly notice the passing of time as it stretches across the floor and forget my fretfulness completely during hide-and-go-seek and rounds of song.

("Who'll toll the bell?" "I," said the bull,
"Because I can pull, I'll toll the bell.")
Throughout the city, the church bells sound.

XVII. During supper, I sit in his lap.

I try not to wriggle. I earnestly try. Wriggling makes me seem impatient, which adds to his guilt. My presumed distress makes it difficult for him to touch his meal.

That isn't my intention. I only want his attention. Unimpressed by my behavior, the maid glares as she fills crystal flutes with champagne, but her disapproval does not faze me. Privacy is a concept I put little stock in.

I spiral contentedly atop his thighs.

The Lady is lovelier than ever in the smoldering candlelight: young and vibrant, skin supple and cheeks glowing. Her wedding had swollen her heart with joy, and that had swollen her bosom, too. She lifts her glass towards her husband and proposes a toast.

"To our happiness. To the happiness of our families. And to the happiness of the family... that we will have together."

Her voice is husky, shy. Enchanting. Alcohol bubbles in glasses and veins. He is nervous as well, but still smiles when he reiterates:

"To family."

⸺⬥⸺

XVIII. The bedchamber is dark. I can move as I please.

Excited, I race on ahead, slipping between ankles and flying over floorboards. I roll atop the coverlet. I spin around the posters, fold into the curtains, bounce atop the mattress.

I turn and find the Master and the Lady have hesitated in the threshold. Behind them, the maid looms, her brow arched.

"Once upon a time not terribly long ago, outside parties were required to pay witness to a couple's first night together," she comments, her monotone painfully professional. "Comparatively, this shouldn't be nearly as embarrassing, I don't think."

The Master splutters. His flusterment visibly charms his new wife, who relaxes when he grumbles, "You're not helping."

The maid's expression betrays nothing.

"Does my Lord *need* help to... get the job done?"

"No."

The newlyweds enter the room, walking directly towards me.

———⋅◦⋅———

XIX. The ribbons in her hair hiss when unwoven, almost like flames being snuffed. Curls tumble around slender shoulders, their waves swept away by a hand. This gives her husband better access to the cords that crisscross down her back.

He presses a dry kiss to her nape, his fingers tangling in the knots.

(*"Who'll carry the coffin?" "I," said the Kite,*

"If it's not through the night, I'll carry the coffin.")

A dress and a petticoat fall to the floor. The Lady steps out of them as one would a fairy ring, her toes delicately pointed. Fanciful murmurings—vows and dreams and pretty things that I can only catch parts of—slur together on the tip of her tongue, because he is kissing her, kissing her fiercely, and she is losing oxygen and strength and her train of thought.

They fall back on the eiderdown, twisting like I did. I watch them from the pillows, enthralled by all the ways that she is beautiful, and pliant, and trapped between the Master's thighs, gazing trustingly up at him as he pins her wrists to the blankets.

He returns her smile. Touches his mouth to her forehead. Whispers, "Now."

———⋅◦⋅———

XX. The Lady does not realize something is wrong until she feels me in her trachea, lodged like a lump of undigested food.

Instinctively, she chokes. Keens. Surely struggles against her husband, hips jerking and eyes bulging, but his grip remains firm. He is unmoved.

I do not move, either. Not *up*, not *out*. I endure esophageal contractions, wait for painful spasms to subside, then tear my way purposefully *down*, skittering along ribbed muscles as an insect would. Or a parasite.

I am not a parasite.

I tumble into her belly with a splash of acid. For a moment, I sit in that puddle, dazed and trembling, listening to the rhythm of an unseen heart, to the undulating rumble of intestines. Blood rushes through tubers and capillaries.

It is warm here. Pleasant. Familiar? The same.

We are the same. The blood, the bile, the helixing bits. We are compatible.

Family.

My essence uncoils, tentative. Feeling. I feel, and am felt, and am doing the feeling. I can breathe. I can *breathe.* Her lungs are mine. I want to *clutch* them, *squeeze*—

No. No, wait. I need them.

Be gentle.

I pet them. They are porous and soft. Like the cushions in the parlor, she is soft all over. And still warm. Soft and warm.

I like her very much.

And so, I fill her, slowly, with wisps and vines of Self. I spiral downward to thread through ligaments. I loop upward to coat her bones. Every nerve and artery and lipid is prodded, catalogued, assimilated. I feel so happy. She feels so frightened.

Oh dear.

Her mind resists me. Her soul fights.

But a doll has no need for minds or souls.

———◦———

XXI. I am a Covenant.

I am *their* Covenant. I am a vow that bound two into one, born from hatred and desire and corruption and something depraved that twisted into something profound.

I am the soul that a witch sold for power.

I am the lives that a greedy count sacrificed.

I am their spawn, their sins personified, their squandered chance to relearn humanity, to remember that love lets go.

He does not let her go. I do not let her go.

We love—we *love*—and we do not let go.

———◦———

XXII. He is above me.

He is speaking.

He is above me and is speaking and I can *feel* him, I can *hear* him, as I never have before, from specified points of pressure and contact. His hands are no longer bound around her, around *me*— but I can feel where they'd been clutching. My wrists are sore, and my legs are tired. She must have thrashed more than I'd realized.

He speaks again. Words. Language. I know words and language. As did she. She kept her words and language in her brain. Her brain should tell me—

Ah. I ate her brain. I put my knowledge in it instead. Where did I put that knowledge? I rifle and rummage as he speaks a third time. Maybe I can read his lips...? No, I cannot see. Why can't I see?

My eyes are closed.

Oh.

At once, I snap them open. There is little light, for it is still night, but the candle-fire burns with a fierceness I did not expect. My pupils dilate, and the wet film between the balls and the lids replenish themselves as I blink once, twice, three times.

"—yn...?"

His voice echoes out of his chest, unexpectedly deep. Soft. Humans are so *soft*. His face is soft, too, as if seen through hoar. Its details are blurry and underdefined. Only when I remember how to utilize my corneas do he and his worries come into focus.

I realize he is saying my name.

"—ryn...?"

He sees *me.*

Though it takes concentrated effort, I pinch the corners of my lips. I lift them. They skim the flesh of his knuckle, tasting soap and sweat, and I am smiling. I am *smiling*. He can see me, and he cares, and I am *smiling*.

The Master's breath hitches. The gasp of it wedges in his throat, fluttering like a pulse. Like wings.

"Aderyn?" he repeats, fingers unfurling along the curve of my—*my*—face. "Aderyn, is that you?"

Response. Answer. Words. Language. Knowledge. Yes. Yes.

"Yes," I tell him. My own voice resounds in my ears, in my head, in the room. It is loud and reverberating. It is startling, but I am too elated to be alarmed.

I want to make more noises. I want to move my tongue and my limbs. I want to touch. I want to *do*.

I suck down another mouthful of air. It tastes of wax and smoke, makeup and hot skin. I move my arm-elbow-hand jerkily, carefully, to cover his own.

I say again, "Yes, Father."

XXIII. I receive many compliments.

The Master tells me I am beautiful. The maid tells me she is proud. She joins us sometime later, and we three lay atop the bed, my heart beating so fast I am afraid it will break through my breast. Ribcage shattered, blood everywhere. Another ruined body.

When I speak of these fears, my sires laugh.

"You were brave."

"You did well."

They kiss each other, then kiss me. Different kisses. I like mine better.

I like *being* better.

I feel so much *better*. But though I am no longer sick, the Master says I am.

"My poor cousin," he laments at a gathering, sighing into his wineglass as I nurse a cordial at his side. "Her memories are gone. Victim to a new wife's stress, I expect."

Behind us, the maid feigns remorse. Violet eyes flash. The shock of the pronouncement comes and goes like a draft, the chill it elicited forgotten within moments.

She is like a different person, the guests say in a hush, hiding behind gloves and ornate fans. Old friends marvel at the change, and family members gawk. They debate my transformation as if I could not hear them before ultimately deciding, *Perhaps this is for the best. The Lady was always a bit... well. How like a doll she is now! Graceful, demure, and poised.*

Concerns are dismissed. The scandal breezes over. A murder of crows screech outside.

("Who'll sing a psalm?" "I," said the Thrush
"As she sat on a bush, I'll sing a psalm.")

She is not missed.

⸺⸺◦⸺⸺

XXIV. I always wanted to sing with her.

Now, I can. I do.

We chant nursery rhymes that harmonize with the church bells, our sweet voice fluting high. Swooping low. Using the window as a mirror, I brush the blonde curls of my favorite doll, the brunette and the redhead watching on in jealousy.

The cradle and its load have vanished. Time is stopped by my shadow.

I am alive.

Beyond frosted glass, a sparrow flits from a dead tree.

⸻ ◆ ⸻

*XXV. (All the birds of the air fell a-sighing and a-sobbing,
When they heard the bell toll for poor Cock Robin.)*

*Major Key Inspiration:
"Who Killed Cock Robin"*

iv. a bunch of flowers for your life

0. Your first word is the most important, and your first word is this:

"Dandelion."

The demigod pauses where he stands, his great mass looming and his ageless face smooth. Stood beneath his golden shears, you bear the mark of a target: a gilded X that hovers above your head, casting sickle shadows. Your soul quavers.

But you have not been cut down yet.

To your left, your brethren lie in a long, limp line, arms knotted and bodies crumpled. Neatly culled, they slouch one atop the other atop the other atop the other, an early spring breeze making vines of their hair. Those tendrils creep, quiet. With eyes wide open, they dream a dream eternal atop a soft soil bed.

You curl your toes in your ancestors, soon to be your peers.

"Dandelion," you say again, even as the canopy claps and snickers at you, throwing back echoes of earlier declarations: *rose* and *orchid*, *trillium* and *hurricane lily*. Branches join in, guffawing until they groan, as they remind you of *spring cress* and *columbine* and *forget-me-nots*. They laugh and laugh.

The demigod does not laugh.

He lowers his shears.

⸺◆⸻

You are not sure what to do with life now that you have it. You trail after him, an acolyte seeking answers.

"You can eat me," you offer, edging along an unforged path. "Or make me into wine. I'd taste good for you, I promise."

He says nothing, walking on. A butterfly has alighted upon his sublime cheek, lazily beating diaphanous wings. From afar, a chickadee calls for its sweetie.

"Would you like to boil me for tea?"

The demigod pauses. Stands, noble, betwixt shadows and light, open space and closed, the woods and a meadow in its dramatic summer throes.

You gaze across that field as well. It sprawls, an inverted sky beneath your feet. Here, the horizon. There, the meteors. Bush-planets pocked with floral craters are orbited by a Milky Way stream, its surface dotted in stars that wink in the afternoon's liminal light. Space expands before you, and lo—in asterisms and asteroids embedded in the dirt—swirl a hundred million suns in potent-pollen galaxies, brightening dark earth with their radiance.

You are brilliant. That brilliance touches everything.

He glances at you from over his magnificent shoulder, and you understand that you were chosen.

But *why*?

⸺◆⸻

Days go by, then months, then seasons.

You meander in the demigod's wake, adorning his glorious head with butter-bloom diadems and his sanctified throat with chain-linked necklaces. The yellow that stains his resplendent nose is almost permanent now. Your fingertips match.

Across grasslands, over mountains, the pair of you wander. You see yourself in shades of day and night and dusk, and you see him in mists and dewdrops and rainstorms.

There are other cullings. Nostalgic, you watch its candidates rise up, file up, make up their cases before him: *rose, orchid, trillium, hurricane lily. Spring cress, columbine, forget-me-nots.*

Sometimes, they are heard and survive. Sometimes, they are dismissed and pruned. Sometimes, they are absent entirely, replaced by *daffodil, jack-in-the-pulpit, bleeding hearts, morning glory.*

Always, they come and go and live and die.

Never do they follow.

You are the only one.

* * *

"Finished," decrees the demigod, his brontide whisper sweeping across the land. From sea to sea and top to bottom, the wilderness releases a collective sigh. It is both communal and communion, an exhalation that rustles his furs.

You blink. "Sir?"

"They will be arriving soon," he tells you. A sliver of moonlight peeks through his divine smile, sharp as any set of shears. "Another change to our landscape. In the aftermath, little one, I too will need to change. But you will serve them well for me, will you not? You will welcome them, and care for them, and add beauty to their short lives. And in return, once they have died, you and yours shall feast. You will thrive upon their remains."

He looks at you in all his majesty, shoulders squared and antlers glistening and countless, bead-black eyes shining like the cosmos. His beauty overwhelms, and creamy tears drip down your face.

You wish to do all he asks. You wish to reject his desires. You wish to be what he loves.

You wish, you wish, you *wish*.

"If that is your wish," you vow, "I will do my best to grant it."

Perfect lips grace your crown. A breath—singular and warm, sweet and excruciating—bursts against your now-blessed brow.

You burst along with it. Heart-mind-soul divided into fragments, you drift away on the wind to set roots elsewhere.

"Then off you go."

⋯⋯◇⋯⋯

i. "In another life," he sniffs, "I was treated like a god."

Rosebay, marigold, and cypress sprigs make for a unique arrangement, equal parts macabre and vibrant. Green brings out orange, and orange complements violet. Sterile walls intensify the vivacity of all colors. Feathering out the cramped blossoms would do nothing to save them from choking in their bottleneck, so you don't bother trying.

A lingering whiff of coffee clings to the rim of the glass. It wrinkles your nose.

"You mean you *would've* been treated like a god," you correct.

"No." Adamant, the man on the bed sniffs again, scrubbing his knuckles beneath his right nostril. It comes away plated, a glistening sheen smudged over liver spots. "I mean I *was*. I remember."

"You don't."

"I *do*," he insists, fist slamming weakly atop his white comforter. It rumples his white sheets and makes the white mattress squeak. There is so little that is not white in this antiseptic space. Himself pale to the point of translucency, the man pouts and mumbles, "...it *was* just the once, though."

"Mhm."

"Can't always be special. I get that. Sometimes you gotta be a matchmaker with phossy jaw, or a coal miner caught in a collapse. But once, I was a god."

Gold keeps dripping, smelted. Flesh-warmed. Congealing into ingots. If the janitor could see spiritual residue, they would be mortified. Even knowing they can't, you don't envy them their job.

The clock on the bedside table ticks. You shrug in the most pacifying way that you are able. "Okay. Sure. I mean, I wasn't there, so. You'd know better than me."

"Damn right I would." He coughs, upsetting one of his machines. "I just... I can't believe I didn't remember until now. It's like forgetting you used to play baseball until going to see a game. Then it all suddenly comes rushing back."

"Memories are strange, ephemeral things."

"Yeah, I guess."

Neither of you say anything for a bit, content to watch a purple floret detach itself and float idly to the tabletop. There, it is welcomed by the corpses of other fallen petals, offered a resting place in their mass grave.

You think there could be a metaphor in that. In the slow demise of the rosebay stalk, paired with the quicker deaths of its individual blooms.

Probably. If you wanted to find it.

"...eh. What does it matter, anyway." The man sighs into your shared silence, touching a finger to the ichor that flows from his body. Sunset grants it a metallic gleam. His hand shines. Holding it up, palm-out, to slatted windows, he considers his own failing design, each tic and spasm reminding you of an automaton winding down. "The gods are dead, they say. Makes sense that there'd be no saving me, either."

"Oh, c'mon," you scoff, rolling your eyes at his sulk. "It's nothing as personal as that. It's a matter of entropy."

When he snorts, it pops a bubble in his secretions.

"Being alive *does* take the energy out of you, I'll give you that."

"Look. For what it's worth," you tell him, "there *was* talk of putting you in another body. Thought you might have one more life left in you. A short one, mind, like maybe a stillbirth. But, yeah. Then the math got double-checked."

He hums like he knows what you're talking about. Maybe he does. Who's to say? Despite your familiarity with death, you have not been in his position before.

Still, you have a heart with which to empathize. You do your best to make use of it.

"So. What's next for me?" the man in the gilt-smeared bed asks, molten fluid oozing down his cheek now, too. "Or, you know, whatever's left of me. When a soul can't be a soul anymore, what does it become? Am I to be... nothing?"

How unfortunate it is, humanity's fear of the unknown. Why wire that into them, you've always wondered, when they hardly know anything at all? If only you'd had the foresight to ask.

As it is...

"I think," you say, one eye on the clock and the other on the bouquet, "that you're going to be everything."

Beneath his funerary shroud of years and skin and ectoplasm, the man has a nice smile. You're glad that's what he's wearing when he goes.

8:03 PM.

The dribbling stops.

In between instants, the hospital room transforms, evolving into a provisional tomb. The cypress's presence is made appropriate as the rosebay surrenders its last buds. Finally, the marigolds overpower the bittersweet aroma of their pseudo-vase.

Alarms are sounding. Monitors flash. Neither can detract from the beauty of the moment, the pollen and the particles that helix out the window, elegantly dispersing into the ruddy sky. Nothing can stop this great metamorphosis, this miniaturized Big Bang, and you feel privileged to observe that which cannot be directly observed, even as it itself observes.

We, you have learned, *are at our most basic, a cause, an effect, an assumption, an existence. We are matter that mattered, that*

formed bonds unconditional, and it is by those bonds that we
Become.

It is also by those bonds that you remain. Here, there, connected. By lineage and roots and branches. Separation is a perception, perceptions change with time. Given time, a death god will be no different than a dead god.

In the strangest, most ephemeral recesses of your mind, you see a demigod raise his head. It is a thought that floats away like pappi.

Bracing your elbows on the windowsill, you take a minute to appreciate how exceptionally golden the sunset is tonight.

Then, with no small hunger, you wonder about burial rites.

⸺ ◆ ⸺

It is by bonds that you Become.

It is through severance that you Wither.

The funerals of humans are not the rewards that once they were, and with every passing era the never-ending banquet becomes leaner, sparser, healthy organic sustenance supplemented with ash, and concrete, and formaldehyde.

You do not feast. You do not thrive. You do not even have the energy to burst.

You crumble into dust.

⸺ ◆ ⸺

ii. You take their faces after they are gone.

No one recognizes you behind your masks. No one ever questions you being there, you being *alive*, or confuses you with who you are not. You are too much your own entity, you suppose, too sure of yourself and what you are: everything and nothing, astral leeching from your pores as it does from the tails of shooting stars.

Sometimes, you try to imagine a meteor shower, but can only ever picture a seedhead exploding, its spray streaking across the sky.

No matter. Either scenario would explain why you are wished upon so often.

"Was it worth it? For her, I mean."

Your hair is red where it is tucked behind your ear, curling in the damp of the cemetery. Each wisp is a flame that this autumnal downpour cannot extinguish, though neither does its blaze offer any heat.

You do not offer any heat, either. If you did, the child beside you might not be shivering.

Or maybe he would.

"I don't know," you admit, truthful. You only ever speak in truths. "Worth is a matter of personal perception."

Raindrops spatter between golden leaves, the sound pitched high and low and clear in the afternoon's hush. Your companion hums beside you.

"Then I guess... if you were given the choice that she was," he tries again, "would you make the same decision? Would you give up your... you know... to save yourself?"

You consider your hands—her hands—white and small. You consider the boy—her successor—white and small. You consider the grave—her grave—white and small. Your reflections blur in the waters that sluice over pale marble, leaving you both faceless shadows of what you should be.

"I was given a choice, once," you say to him. Not because you want to, exactly, but because it is another truth. "My... father. He asked me and my siblings to watch over his new children, and I was happy to do so, because I loved him. And because I loved him, I loved them. But because I loved them, I wanted to see them become their best selves. I wanted them to prove to me, to our father, to the *world*, how good they were, how deserving of things. I staged a test. It involved offering one of them something that they should've refused. It should have been so *easy* to refuse."

"But they didn't refuse?"

"They didn't." You look at your hands again. The crown of each tiny finger has turned crimson in the chill. Crimson like her hair, like a flame, like an apple, like your eyes when you confess, "I was furious. I was confused. I was distraught. And it was then that I came to understand my own choice. I could either embrace these children, flaws and all, or ..."

Well.

As you hunch further into your borrowed body, into this plot you have threaded through like weeds, the boy allows the past to trail into the present. Your future is heralded by a long stretch of silence, interrupted only by the serpentine hiss of wind through wet willows.

He sticks his own hands into his pockets. His fists are tight, the size and color of pomegranates, and he swallows before asking, "Why couldn't you accept that they were only human?"

Only human.

You toe at a gifted bouquet of stargazer lilies, cellophane crinkling, petals sodden. They had been grown solely to be killed. To be cut in their prime, when at their most lovely and pitiable.

Only human.

A morbid ritual, giving flowers. Piling corpses atop the dead has always struck you as mockery, but maybe that is your own trauma talking. Maybe, to others, the act is comforting. No one wants to rot alone. Isn't that why the old kings buried themselves with their slaves? Isn't that why men and women were sacrificed to expiring gods? Isn't that why you let yourself be summoned?

Only *human.*

"Because," you whisper, the words weaving into the haze, "they and all the children who came after them, all of you that ever were or ever will be... All of you could—*should*—be so much *more.*"

It is the truth. You only ever speak the truth. You will only ever speak the truth, because in the deepest recesses of your heart, you still want to guide these lost lambs. You still want to save them. Worth is a matter of personal perception, and you want desperately to find worth in humanity again, to look at the boy beside you and see all the power and the wonder, the glory and the honor, hallelujah, hallelujah.

Once upon a time, your line held such high hopes for these mud-born children. But what had those hopes done, besides provide a perch from which to fall?

You hate them. You love them. You believe in them so much more than *he* ever did.

And yet...

The boy beside you smiles. He shouldn't be missing teeth, but he is. He has not told you why.

You know why.

"With your help," he promises, "*I* will be more. I will. I'll be the most and the best that it is possible to be."

Your laugh is the only dry thing in this cemetery. It is a sound smaller than her hands, more pathetic than her flowers.

"No," you correct beneath your breath. "With me by your side, you are already the least and the worst."

"Huh?" He blinks, head cocked to follow the thunder that is rolling above your heads. Strings of black hair are plastered to his cheeks. He asks, "Did you say something?"

You give your new Master a smile of your own: long, and winding, and thin, and unlike his, far too full of teeth. Despite the face you wear, you hardly look human.

It does not matter. No one recognizes you behind your masks.

"Yes," you tell him, truthful. Always truthful. And then, "You look half-starved. Shall we find you something to eat?"

You offer him your hand.

He takes it.

⸻ ❖ ⸻

He takes it. She takes it. They take it.

You take.

You take, and you take, and you take*take*take, until you cannot take anymore. Until you cannot contain anything else.

Until entropy rips you apart.

⸺◈⸺

iii. You're uncertain how many Not Deer there are. Maybe dozens. Maybe millions. Maybe just this one. You could not say from where it came, or how long it has been alive. You try very hard not to linger on what its purpose might be, lest you truly lose your mind. And you can't have that. You can't do that.

You can't.

What you *can* do is recognize this creature when he comes around.

You are willing to admit this skill seems underwhelming. It's not, though. It's impressive. If someone thinks it sounds easy to recognize a Not Deer, that is because they are supposing a Not Deer's appearance lives up to its name.

Whatever it looks like, these imagined people assume, *it must not look like a deer.* It must not have four sinewy legs, a tuft of a tail, two eyes, two ears, and a dark, wet nose. It must not have antlers that bifurcate, as hidden trails do into forests. Depending on the season, its coat will not be thick and coarse, or sparse and thin; its coloring shan't be chocolate-brown, or dusky red, or lustrous umber, or snow-dappled and dull.

The appearance of a mundane deer changes. Based on time, on place. On the specific specimen. But in the end, whatever its details, a deer's silhouette against the rising moon will always be deer-shaped. Which surely means a Not Deer's profile won't be.

But it is.

A Not Deer has four sinewy legs. It has a tuft of a tail, two eyes, two ears, and a dark, wet nose. Its antlers bifurcate, as hidden trails do into forests. Depending on the season, its coat might be thick and coarse, or it could be sparse and thin; its coloring might be chocolate-brown, or dusky red, or lustrous umber, or snow-dappled and dull.

It changes. Based on time, on place. On the specific specimen. But whatever its details, a Not Deer resembles a deer in every conceivable way.

Except, of course, in those ways that it looks nothing like a deer at all.

To you, the distinction is perfectly obvious.

———◆———

The simplest way to recognize a witch, meanwhile, is by their smile.

This is not because they have exceptionally hideous smiles. Far from it. When genuine, no smile is hideous, and you are not so self-deprecating as to think a witch's is the exception to this. But then, by that same token, it would be just as much a lie to call a witch's smile extraordinary.

If it were an extraordinary smile, it would not belong to a witch.

What makes a witch's smile unique is its lack of uniqueness. The smile of a proper witch will be a flawless embodiment of statistical averages. Their mouth will lift on both sides at a fourteen-degree angle, and will stretch no further than the edges of their pupils. It will display eight teeth. Those teeth will be off-white, squarish, and capped by pink gums. Taken as a whole, the expression will be so unremarkable that no one will think to look twice at the witch.

Which is what makes it such a clever disguise.

In your experience, the valley is not an uncanny place, so long as one is willing to ignore those moments when it is.

When the dormant cancers in the shadows' limbs suddenly become malignant, mutating into something monstrous; when the glowworms' plasmatic flickers have transformed the ground into the sky, and the sky into the ground, and the space between is a demimonde of gauzy heat; when it is not day, nor night, nor morning, nor evening, but somewhere in-between, a gray as ambiguous as morality...

When those moments come, you find yourself standing here. The both of you.

And you stare.

The creature, being slightly more bestial than you, lingers around the unkempt outskirts of the woods, its contours congealing with the blues that leach from the twilight. You, being a trifle less human than it, watch from a roiling sea of dew-dappled grass.

A smile is studied. A silhouette scrutinized.

"Well met, little witch," the Not Deer greets, the void of its gaze briefly illumed by fireflies.

Those fireflies blink. It does not.

You nod, tucking a flyaway curl behind your ear.

"Well met," you repeat. "*Auspiciously* met, too, I should hope."

"Oh, most certainly." A Not Deer's smile, unlike a witch's, is terrible in its splendor. Thirteen of its infinite teeth shine in its sweep, quartz stalactites that cling to the mouth of a bleeding cave. Amusement resonates, rumbling from cavernous depths. "On the eve of the estival solstice, how could our meeting be anything *but* auspicious?"

"...indeed." There are charms in your pocket. They are protective and tender. Recently dead. You do not touch them. "In that case, might I assume that our offering appeased?"

"*Your* offering did."

"*My* offering?"

"Oh, all right. I suppose, generously, your contribution might count towards the lives of your family, too."

You both pause at this, assessing the other, bemused by equal and opposing looks of confusion.

"Why are you making such a face?" the Not Deer asks, tilting its head. Because you are quick to brace your feet, you remain upright when the earth tilts in kind. "Surely you are not surprised? No matter the age or the era, a fee only pays for so many, and this is not a village, anymore," it reasons, tapping a hoof thoughtfully against the root of a tree. The sound echoes, treble-sharp, before registering as pain in mortal ears. "T'would be a similar understatement to call this concrete sprawl a *town*. No, it is a *city* that has spawned here, little witch. A ripe and teeming metropolis, brimming with bodies. *Stinking* of hubris. Profligate, leeching, gluttonous."

Understanding hones the cut of your gaze. "You want to rehash the terms of our contract."

"Of your *ancestors'* contract," the Not Deer corrects. Its antlers are like scars carved into the cobalt firmament, barely visible but hideous where they etch timelines into the abyss. As you watch, they fork into the past, branch into the future. If you squint, you can see where clinging sediment separates the Hadean eon from the Archean, the Miocene epoch from the Pliocene. There is a disconcerting freshness to the Holocene nubs that bloom upon its tips. "Things have changed, and I am due my fair share."

"Nothing in this world is *fair*."

"Oh ho. On that, we are agreed. But it is to the human's benefit that you convince me otherwise, lest I prove your own point to those people."

"I see." Contemplative, you fiddle with a forelock, twining the fiery strand around your finger. The red is not natural; you *do* have a soul. Witches, famously, are one of the few mammals who do. You do battle with it, along with your conscience, as you bite your lip and demand, "For what are you asking?"

Long lashes beat. Twice, thrice. Fall is foreshadowed in the dusk's creeping chill, the stench of death and parasitic decay clinging like galls to the underside of the clover-scented breeze.

"There are eight hundred and twenty times more humans here now," the Not Deer muses, "than there were when I first bargained with your forebearers' forebearers. Therefore, in exchange for my continued magnanimity, I would be gifted eight hundred and twenty times as much."

There is no mirth in the bark of your laughter. "That is quite impossible."

"What is impossible is persevering beneath the strain of *so many* greedy inhabitants. My lands are not designed for this. No lands are."

Constellations fade in and out of the Not Deer's stare, prismatic. Ever moving. Its antlers have become an inextricable part of the canopy, integral to its ligneous tangle; the arterial complexity of each spiraling offshoot is reflected in the lacework veins that mar your wrists.

You ponder the brand of those blood ties tattooed beneath your skin before considering your options.

"What if," you wonder, "I give up? What if I break the contract?"

Leaves clap together with the force of a hundred million eyelids. Leg joints flex, evoking thoughts of maggots when they twist and bunch and plicate. For an instant, every firefly winks out, and the glowworms vanish, and the molten remains of the day's last light alchemize from ichor to ink, the world itself guttering as a candle does prior to being snuffed.

Then reality reignites itself. Perceptions shift in synchronization: above, the moon ripples; below, the directions change. Face to face in the tall, tall grass, the titanic Not Deer looms, ever-connected to its primordial forests by a spiderweb of velvet-swathed bones.

It flicks a moth from its left ear.

"You know *exactly* what I would do, little witch."

You do. This knowledge does not stop you from arcing a brow.

"Well then," you drawl, unimpressed by morbid histrionics, "what if I no longer care?"

The Not Deer does not respond. It does not react. You suspect it is unsure how.

"I am... tired," you confess. A shrug accentuates that exhaustion. "I am tired of trying. I am tired of working hard, and striving towards good, and watching so few give a damn. Do you know, when I'm not out here, I'm an environmental engineer? Not that it matters. Be it derived of science or magic, my power only goes so far, and it's killing me. All of this. Figuratively. Literally. So. Why not be the one who breaks the chain, as it were? Why not give up and let nature take its course? Why not sacrifice all unto you?"

The Not Deer's collapsar eyes, as endless as they are ethereal, exert an undeniable gravity upon those who meet its gaze. They find the spirit where it hides in its weak flesh vessel—the shape of it, the incredible mass—and then they pull, pull, *pull*.

"It would not be a sacrifice. Not unto me," the Not Deer says finally. Softly. An antediluvian heat billows from its nostrils, damp with microbes and cyanobacteria. "You cannot sacrifice unto me what is already mine. I fear that you have perhaps misunderstood our arrangement these many years. Allow me to clarify. When those who begot your family tree formed a covenant with me, they did not do so to *stop* anything. The intent was not to *save*, nor to *spare*. The inevitable has always been inevitable, and should you choose not to reestablish their pact, then we shall simply come to that inexorable conclusion slightly earlier than your fellow scientists predicted."

You mull on this. On thoughts of futility, of eternity, with a thumb pressed against your own pulse.

"Is it strange," you chuckle, weary and humorless, "that I find myself thinking about entropy?"

A snort. "I would think it far stranger if you weren't."

There is delicate ceremony to the way that the Not Deer rests its forehead against your own, ruffling your woven dandelion crown. The flowers' weight is roughly comparable to that of thirty thousand lives.

You would know. You have held each one in your hands, at one point or another.

"A wish is a prayer made to chaos," the Not Deer breathes. Its voice is different now, the change as subtle and as dramatic as the turning of the seasons. How unfamiliar this sweetness; how nostalgic and adored. You know it, you realize. You know it. *You know it.* "I no longer have need to pray."

Memories are strange, ephemeral things. And yet, like bonds, they remain. Here, there. A chain that connects you to a hundred million blooms of light.

You have always understood that this creature is not a deer. But only now do you recognize who he is.

Who he *truly* is.

"I did my best," you rasp. It's true. You only ever speak the truth. "I gave it everything I have, everything I am. All of my effort. All of my energy."

"You did," he agrees. "You are the last, you know. I am so proud of you for holding on this long."

His whisper warms the milk and gold that leaches from your eyes, luciferin-bright. You have never known such relief. It is a palpable thing—a self-consuming fire, alive and dying in your breast—and you are radiant with it. Luminous. That brilliance touches everything: brightening dark earth and staining it yellow.

"So I... I can be...?"

"Finished," promises the demigod, his brontide whisper sweeping across the land. From sea to sea and top to bottom, the wilderness releases a collective sigh. It is both communal and communion, an exhalation that rustles his furs.

He inhales. You close your eyes, lips lifting into a smile.

It is extraordinary to behold.

"Off you go, beloved."

And this time, when you burst, the universe follows.

Major Key Inspirations:
Legends of the Not Deer
and the Language of Flowers

v. gnothi seauton

audio tour

(transcript)

*H*ello, I am Anisa McDaniel, the director of collections here at the Museum of Modern Art. On behalf of myself, the museum staff, and the city of New York, I would like to personally thank you for your generous patronage on this, the dawn of our 200th anniversary.

Much has changed since MoMA's inauguration in 1929. Our landscape, our population, our world, is now painted upon a canvas that is vastly different from that which our forefathers would've used on that brisk November day so many decades ago.

What would we look like to them, do you think? What will we look like to our children's children?

Since the epoch of cave paintings, the art world has served as an ever-evolving mirror, warping to reflect the transformations—both ephemeral and literal—that mark the growth of a particular country, person, or era. A body of work can teach us as much about another's beliefs, political views, or cultural standards of beauty as it can shape the way we understand our own fears and loves and losses and tragedies. More than any other medium, art transcends borders: of geography, creed, race. Even temporal strictures. In the immortal words of Longfellow, "Art is long and time is fleeting." Now more than ever, this museum strives to accurately encapsulate the modern human experience, so that we will someday be fully known to our descendants.

In this private, interactive exhibit, Gnothi Seauton, *MoMA has curated a collection that serves not only to define humanity, but to reflect upon its meaning in both the past and future tenses. As one of this museum's premier donors, your audio tour will be led by the incomparable Cezanne Benayoun, creator of the Stedelijk Museum's critically acclaimed* The Body in Art: Redux *installation, and recent winner of the esteemed Academie des Beaux-Arts' Pierre Cardin Award.*

Gnothi Seauton begins on level three, in the special exhibitions wing. Its key works are denoted with golden placards. When seen, simply input the number on the placard into your audio device, then hold the device to your ear to hear Benayoun's narration. Should you experience any technical difficulties, please don't hesitate to ask the staff for assistance.

Once again, from all of us here at MoMA, thank you for choosing to support the arts. We couldn't do this without you.

———— ◆ ————

One. "Selections from the Cave Paintings of Lascaux." Originally discovered in 1940.

Previously displayed in the Field Museum, these Paleolithic paintings depict life as it was on the proverbial cusp, when our ancestors' naked, hominoid feet straddled the line between savagery and discipline, culture and chaos. Art historians suggest that it was towards the end of this period that our forefathers first began to express themselves on rock walls, leaving the impressionistic scenes of long-extinct equines and aurochs that you now see before you.

To this day, no consensus has been reached as to the meaning behind these images. Some argue that they are remnants of ritual. Others, that they illustrate long-forgotten stories. What can be agreed upon are the scientific details: that these yellows, reds, and blacks were created from a complex assortment of iron and manganese compounds. Minerals which someone had to have harvested from the earth, that magical place from whence all things come, and all life goes.

We are art, in that sense. Humans are masterpieces mid-progress.

Therefore, it is interesting to note that, in spite of being so perfectly incomplete—or, perhaps, *because* of it—out of the two thousand pictographs catalogued in Grotte de Lascaux, only one is of a man.

Is he a man?

Look, then squint. Squint, then blink. Blink, then look again. Wonder. This figure, this creature, who for untold millennia hid in the pitch-dark of the Great Fissure—does he provide us with answers about our collective past, or does he ask more questions? What do we know about him? He is elongated, splayed, his arms spread wide and his features unmistakably avian. He is dead, or dying, or in the midst of an apotheotic metamorphosis. He is one of a mere eight images found in the cavern's now famed shaft, and three of those are but geometric signs, microbial and meaningless.

After coming to personal conclusions about an antediluvian stick figure, I would invite you to visit the adjacent chalk wall, where previous patrons have, in homage, scrawled their own interpretive likenesses. Take a few minutes to add your face, in your hand, in whatever colors are most representative of you. Erase others' pictures as necessary. Remember, all is transience.

[*FIVE MINUTES OF RICHARD STRAUSS' "META-MORPHOSEN" PLAYS. FADES.*]

Are you still drawing? I hope that you are. I hope that you have noticed the opaque odor of your chalk; that you are appreciating the soft, gritty feel of processed limestone mixing with your sweat; that you are considering your life and reliving the intricate series of serendipitous misfortunes that brought you here, to this moment.

I hope that you are not thinking about those other pictures you might have erased. You only did what was necessary.

Take five more minutes. Remember, all is transience, but brevity is relative.

[*RICHARD STRAUSS' "METAMORPHOSEN" CON-TINUES. FADES.*]

When you have finished with your portrait, I invite you to step back. Look, squint, blink, look again at what you have done. Wonder: Do you recognize yourself on the wall? Do you understand yourself in the context of those who came before you? Do you comprehend your contribution when taken out of that context? How do you compare? Do you compare? Should you compare?

Look, squint, blink, look again. Wonder.

Who is that?

Look, squint, blink, look again. Wonder.

Who are you?

[*TONE*]

———◆———

Two. "Mixed Blessing." Multiple artists. Assembled by Leon Papadopoulos in 2030.

Since time immemorial, theologians, politicians, religious leaders, and numerous fantasy novelists have sustained careers on claims that a battle is being ever waged between the ouroboros forces of good and evil. In this stylized hospital room, you will find a manipulatable database of this battle's most eminent warriors.

We are born and die in blood.

Being cautious of the step, place yourself behind the central console. Don't be shy about it. Once the floor sensors register your presence, the installation will turn on automatically. This process will take no more than 30 seconds.

[*30 SECONDS OF SILENCE.*]

After they have finished loading, feel free to peruse the archives at your leisure. This catalogue features over 8,000 years' worth of antagonists and champions. For a few moments, consider the effort required to satisfactorily compile so much information, and bask in genuine awe.

[*30 MORE SECONDS OF SILENCE.*]

Leon Papadopoulos—himself part theologian, part novelist—spent over half his career locating, excavating, recreating, dimensioning, and digitizing depictions of history's most illustrious characters. Arguably, this catalogue could be considered a masterpiece in itself, but to force such a perspective would be a disservice to both its artist and its audience.

Continue to scroll through the database. Appreciate the multiple lenses—both physical and figurative—that Papadopoulos needed to use to present each image in such stunning definition. Admire, just to begin, the foundational pieces displayed in the footnotes. Qin Shi Huang's beautiful silk portraits, colorized photographs of Chiune Sugihara, rare video of Humaira Ahmad. Take another minute to acknowledge how completely impossible it is to wrap your brain around the reality that once—many, many years ago—these facts and famous portraits were real, breathing people: people who experienced itchy ankles and private embarrassments and unrequited affections, who had blemishes and favorite jokes and cried when they felt alone.

When you are ready, touch an avatar that interests you. The applicable hologram will appear on Dais One, the black platform to your left. After it has rendered fully, go ahead and touch its arm, or its foot. Cup its cheek. Tell yourself that you can feel each pore on its face, every strand of peach-fuzz on its chin.

Tell yourself this because it is true.

Choose a second avatar from the database. This one will project itself onto Dais Three, the white platform on your right. Once its extremities have congealed, caress its elbow, prod its belly. Tell yourself that the bones in its mouth are real, rather than brittle and broken and lost forever to time.

Tell yourself this because it is not true.

Do you tell yourself many things that are not true?

Many, many things?

In the final years of his life, Papadopoulos opened up considerably about his childhood—a famously tumultuous era of human history—and how the monotheistic culture of the day inspired his later work. As he noted in his 2068 bestseller, *Genocide/Genesis*:

"[...] any holy tome composed in black ink on white paper inflicts on its reader psychological harm. After all, pragmatically, purest dark and purest light do precisely the same thing: they blind."

In Papadopoulos's experience, the extremes touted by the most prevalent religions of the early twenty-first century bred into their followers a "black and white mentality" that, at best, he found unrealistic, and at worst provided a foundation for a majority of the world's intolerances.

Intolerance did not prove a foundation upon which a healthy society could be built.

During the course of this narration, where have your eyes been? Have you been looking at the Daises? Have you been concerned, maybe—alarmed, maybe—to see the holograms' scalps lift cleanly off projected skulls? To watch arms detach, soundlessly, from socket-ball joints? You can break their limbs into smaller pieces, if you wish. You could break these renderings into their basest molecules. Do you think, if you did, you could find the root of evil? The chromosomes that hide divinity?

From Dais One and Three, select what pieces or parts you prefer, then assemble them on Dais Two, centered and gray. Use the console to change your selected avatars whenever you desire. Take a nose from one projection, then a rib from the second.

Help yourself to the calves of Czar Ivan IV, the kneecap of Guru Arjan, the middle-left toe of Elvinia Milford Espinoza, the right index knuckle of Countess Elizabeth Báthory de Ecsed. Whoever, whenever, whatever.

As you create this body, contemplate the equally unbalanced, erratic, and imperfect creation that is your own. Consider the men and women who lived and died and lived and died and lived and died and lived and died, so that you, too, could live and die. You are the genetic equivalent of the telephone game.

Listen. What convoluted message spirals through your DNA?

[*FIVE MINUTES OF RICHARD STRAUSS' "META-MORPHOSEN" PLAYS. FADES.*]

[*TONE*]

⸺⸺◆⸺⸺

Three. "Weight," 2101. Zahra Aziz-Sawyer.

In the year 1907, a physician from Haverhill, Massachusetts named Duncan MacDougall published a study entitled the 21 Gram Experiment. In his work, MacDougall postulated that the weight of the average human soul is approximately twenty-one grams, a conclusion drawn by measuring the body mass of a small number of tuberculosis patients just-before and just-after their last breaths.

Deemed flawed and unscientific even during the age in which it was printed, the experiment's results were ultimately, and unsurprisingly, rejected by the scientific community at large. However, the idea of a twenty-one-gram soul gained a cult of fanciful proponents throughout the course of subsequent centuries, and has since featured in many popular movies, books, podcasts, and sim-sertions. More relevantly, it served as half the inspiration behind Egyptian contemporary artist Zahra Aziz-Sawyer's masterpiece, "Weight."

In an interview conducted for the purposes of this audio guide, Aziz-Sawyer stated that her goal with "Weight," as with so many of her other pieces, was to amalgamate the modern and the bygone, the then and the now, the audience and the art.

[ZAHRA AZIZ-SAWYER'S VOICE:] "We are all a sum of our parts. Parts that are bloated, falling into rot. That are cursed by their own actions, or—more likely—by their own inactions. And if our parts are damned, what else can our sums be? There is no such thing as salvation."

Holding carefully to the rail, proceed to climb into the empty half of "Weight's" metalwork scale balance. During the twenty-one seconds it takes for judgement to be wrought, marvel at the impossible, ethereal beauty of the heavens painted above you. Wonder at how inviting they seem, how soft and peaceful. Then—

Feel the air rush past you, out of your lungs, as your basket drops unceremoniously to the hellfire floor. Notice your breath as it leaves you with the juddering, discomforting finality it would a tuberculosis patient.

Was that your soul?

Take a breath, if you can. Keep trying until you succeed. Remember other breaths that you have taken, air that you have used. Air that you have wasted, have spent on condemning others, or dismissing a stranger's suffering. On telling them that you have no money, no food, no water to offer.

How much did each of those breaths weigh, do you think?

If they weighed nothing, what does that say about you?

[*TONE*]

Four. "Annihilation in A Minor," 2126. Rayyan Balogh.

Before his incarceration and subsequent execution, Rayyan Balogh gained notoriety in his home country for staging an impassioned crusade against what he saw as systemic corruption in the ruling regime. Like many other artists, Balogh sought to further his cause and his message through his work. Unlike many other artists, Balogh enjoyed a degree of success before his governmentally sanctioned demise.

Anyone with a taste for contemporary art is surely familiar with Balogh's most renowned work, "House," which stood in the Iparművészeti Múzeum for two months. Which is to say, it stood in the Iparművészeti Múzeum until thrown stones reduced the famed installation's walls to a powder so impossibly fine that health risks became a major concern. Indeed, in the piece's final days, there were no less than four confirmed cases of visitors requiring medical assistance for ground glass in the lungs.

Let us now, together, think about the lungs. While humans are not alone in having them, our species is certainly unique in our willingness to endanger them.

What color is the air outside today? What color was it when "Annihilation in A Minor" was first created? What color will it be when "Annihilation in A Minor" returns to nothingness?

Take a breath. Feel that oxygen sit, heavy and putrid, on the back of your tongue. Swallow, if necessary. Force that breath into your lungs, then stand still and know that "Annihilation in A Minor" has permeated your bloodstream.

Take another breath. Slow, slimy, thick. But this time, focus not on the air's assault to your senses, but rather the delicate melancholia of the melody. The fragility of sallow keys, gutted of marrow. The strained and snapping sinew attached to the organ. It's soulful, isn't it? A song with weight. Grams of it. It might haunt you, this song. Will it haunt you?

Take one last breath. Realize, as so many patrons before you have realized, that "Annihilation in A Minor" is now an inextricable part of you, much as "House" was an inextricable part of four of its admirers.

The air we breathe, the water we drink, the food we eat, the DNA in our genetic sequences. These are an inextricable part of you, much as they were an inextricable part of the people who used them before you.

We are inextricable parts of one another.

We are all a sum of our parts.

[*TONE*]

Five. "Self-Im(age)molation," 2129. Multiple artists. Assembled by Anisa McDaniel.

The Delphic maxim *"gnothi seauton,"* translated into English as "know thyself," was allegedly expounded upon by the philosopher Socrates at the time of his trial. When given the opportunity to pick between execution and exile, Socrates decreed that "the unexamined life is not worth living" before making the noble choice to die, rather than face a less honorable—and more horrible—alternative.

Once again, on behalf of Anisa McDaniel, the museum staff, and all those who create and consume the arts, we offer our most heartfelt thanks for the generous donation that you are about to make to MoMA. When given the opportunity to pick, you made the noble choice.

With your left foot, take your first step into the darkness. Follow through with your right. Do this again. Then again. In time, there will be noises. I will dampen them for you. There will also be smells. I can do less to assist with those.

Don't forget, this *is* preferable to the alternative.

Pray, if it helps. Cry, if you'd rather. Argue that the greatest talents have been frequently misapplied and have produced evil proportionate to the extent of their powers. Recite to yourself that silly Goethe poem from your school days:

Niemand wird sich selber kennen,
Sich von seinem Selbst-Ich trennen;
Doch probier' er jeden Tag,
Was nach außen endlich, klar,
Was er ist und was er war,
Was er kann und was er mag.

However you decide to spend these moments, when you pass the designated basket, please remember to return this audio guide.

We dedicate this final installation to the memory of Thomas Robert Malthus.

[*FIVE MINUTES OF RICHARD STRAUSS' "META-MORPHOSEN" PLAYS. FADES.*]

[*TONE*]

Major Key Inspiration:
"Metamorphosen"

vi. fps

Canace is the first to go missing.

He does not notice right away. No one does. It may be a private forum that Act is running, but "private" is not the same thing as "small." There are, at any given time, anywhere between seven and ninety-three members to be monitoring, and it's not as if he has any direct knowledge of or control over these people.

Interests wax and interests wane. Members come and go accordingly. Communal hobbies may create a special sort of bond between online strangers, but those connections are not always strong enough to survive preexisting obligations or sudden changes in schedules.

At the end of the day, Act is a moderator, not a babysitter.

But then Pterelas stops posting. And Hylactor. And Therodamas, all of whom had been regulars on the forum for years, and all in such immediate succession that Act half-wonders if they were in the same freak accident. Or were collectively incapacitated. Or were somehow, simultaneously, spirited away. There is to Agre's final post a half-finished quality that makes Act wonder if she had been kidnapped mid-sentence. If her hitting that last *return* had been both a mistake and an instance of terrible, horrible irony.

Something is *happening*, Act is certain of it. Something is *changing*; he can feel it in his bones.

Something is *wrong*.

"Oh, come on. That's a bit tinfoil hat, isn't it?" Lys laughs, looking away from her own setup of monitors and keyboards to level Act a wry stare. "Look. I know you're worried about our internet friends. And that's sweet, sure, but it's barely been—what, a month? People go on vacation, you know? It's summer. Not everyone is as invested in gaming and design and stuff as we are."

"Yeah, but—"

"Act, we're not, like, running a political activist group, here. Or some special subsection of Anonymous, or whatever," Lys drawls, eyes rolling back to her screen. Whatever new program she has been working so diligently on blinks, its unfinished java strings green and long and complicated. "I can think of exactly zero reasons why someone would go through the trouble of, I dunno, abducting our ragtag group of *nerds* in the middle of the night. Now calm down, you're making *me* nervous. And when I'm nervous, I can't work efficiently. Which means I'll be taking my anger out on *you* if I wind up behind schedule."

"But you're *always* behind schedule."

"Then you should probably chill, huh? Before you make everything worse."

"*Or* you could not act like a massive jerk. For *once*," Act grumbles, glaring at his bank of computers. Still, he allows the conversation to drop.

At least, the conversation that he is having with Lys, in person.

What he posts about online isn't really his twin's business. Even if, technically, Lys is a site admin.

Google News Update:

Will learning to code the human brain offer... (CNN.com)
10 video games IMPROVED by VR graphics and... (YouTube)
New FPS survival launch promises to... (GamesRadar)
3 dead and 1 missing after gruesome... (The Oregonian)

4 wat its worth i tink ur onto sumthig, Tigris says in a DM, his message the usual mess of shorthand, misspellings, and disregarded grammar. Part of Act will always find this sort of carelessness annoying, but the other part of him is weirdly comforted by Tigris's familiar illegibility, given the state of things. If nothing else, Act can be reasonably sure that Tigris is the one who wrote this, rather than whatever mysterious power may or may not be behind their fellows' disappearances. *i hvnt herd back frum thoos in lyke 5 weeks n usuallly i cant make him stfu about w/e erly review hes got and lacon n ladon hvnt posted on YT in 2 mnths. i thnk its th gov.*

I highly doubt the government has anything to do with this, Act writes in reply, Lys's commentary returning to him in a rush of frustration and second-hand embarrassment. At least Tigris hadn't posted his conspiracies publicly. Knowing his luck, Lys would have seen it before he'd had a chance to run damage control, and Act would never have heard the end of it. *Lacon and Ladon are probably busy with sponsors. And weren't they getting into doing early reviews, too? Maybe there's some nondisclosure thing that has kept them from uploading.*

Written out, it seems plausible. Sort of. Act really is trying to be rational about this; he may be worried, but he is not paranoid. He refuses to be paranoid.

Tigris's response comes less than ten seconds after Act hits *enter.* One of the benefits of never proofreading, Act supposes.

yah lacon an ladon got a coopy of wat thoos wuz playn an i thnk hylactor to? sum new big vr upgrade thats supoosed too ""revolutionize"" the fps xperience

Act squints for a few moments, parsing meaning from the message. *What sort of VR upgrade?* he shoots back. *I haven't read anything on the blogs, or heard anything announced?*

dunno u no all I do.

Thoos didn't mention the company who sent him the early review copy? And wait, is it an "upgrade" to an existing VR system or an actual, early review copy of some new first-person shooter? There's a difference.

dude i told u. u no wat i do, Tigris says again, sounding as snippy as one is able when communicating via text. *i can try 2 dm him about it but i wuldnt hold ur breath for an ansr.*

Thanks. I won't.

And it is a good thing that he doesn't. Not only does Act never get an answer from Thoos, but he stops hearing from Tigris, too.

⸺⬦⸺

Google News Update:

Violent serial murders in Oregon catching national... (The Guardian)
Programing urban legends: cryptid codes that... (WhatCulture)
Top 5 MOST SAVAGE fighting VR arenas... (YouTube)
"Like he was ripped apart by an animal." 22 dead and 8 missing in... (The New York Times)

⸺⬦⸺

It is never a good sign when Lys turns fully from her work.

"Act," she sighs, going so far as to cross her arms over her chest and glare. "Come on. Please. You're starting to freak *me* out with your... obsession. About this. People *leave*, okay? It happens. They get busy or they get bored and they leave. There isn't some grand scheme playing out in the shadows, you know? It's just... it's *life.*"

"Is it, though?" Act counters, aiming for vehement but landing closer to panicked. "Is it? Because—because look, I *know* it's the internet, and no one uses their real names, but when you start comparing dates and location details to... to some of the stuff that's been on the news, lately—"

He cuts himself off with a quiet yelp when his laptop screen nearly closes on his fingers. Startled, Act looks up to find Lys looming over his desk, her crown of dark curls shining against the backlight of over-bright technology.

"Okay," she announces, "that's enough of that, Sherlock Holmes. Time for a distraction, I think."

"Lys, I don't want—"

"Tough," she sings, grabbing his fist and dragging. It does not even matter that Act refuses to stand; the wheels on his chair betray him, and he is rolled easily enough before the complicated mess of processors, wires, and docks that make up Lys's workspace. "I've been looking for someone new to alpha test this project I've been working on, and wouldn't you know? I've just found the perfect candidate!"

"Oh. Joy," Act groans, but does not otherwise resist as the VR headset is slipped over his eyes. If anything, the added weight justifies his slumping. "And this *perfect candidate* will be doing what, exactly?"

"Hmm," Lys thinks for a moment, hitting a series of keys. "A lot of running, probably?"

"Not in a *headset,* I won't be."

"Ha! No," Lys agrees, as the display before Act's eyes winks to life. It is not particularly creative, as digital worlds go; just murky, liquid blackness wherein symbols occasionally breach, their message slipping in and out of reality in phantasmagoric polychrome: διεσπάσαντο. διεσπάσαντο. διεσπάσαντο. "Don't worry, the headset becomes irrelevant pretty quick. Just need it to... get things started, I guess?"

The lack of a reference point on which to focus is making this whole experience both vertiginous and uncannily hypnotic. Act tries to close his eyes against the surging simulation sickness, but doing so accomplishes nothing. The message seeps through his lids like blood through tissue, and it all begins again: tenebrous, kaleidoscopic, διεσπάσαντο, leaching through his membranes and imprinting somewhere deeper. There is the thought of retinal scans, but no—Act does not think he is being *read*, exactly.

It is more like he is being written. Rewritten.

"L-Lys...? Lyssa, I—I don't like... I feel—I *feel*...?"

"Yeah. Yeah, I'm sure you do," Lys sympathizes, if cheerfully, as she uses her own hands to shackle Act's shuddering wrists to the chair's armrests. "I've gotten that feedback a lot. Not much for it, I'm afraid. Since that's kind of the point."

"Wha—"

"I call this the ARTificial EMotional Immersion System. Or ARTEMIS, for short. It... encourages? Exacerbates? Let's go with *exacerbates*—certain *passions* in exposed players. Gets the blood pumping, as it were. Taps into the lizard brain and really turns it *on*. My hope is to return *meaning* to so many inane, pointless games. Humanity has really made a mockery of its roots, you know? But I won't go on about that. I'm a programmer, not a poet."

Act feels his mouth open, hears a noise come out of it. It sounds ill. Confused. Animalistic.

"There are different modes, of course," Lys continues, her long, fettering fingers pressing bruises into Act's skin, "and I've had plenty of people help me test the proverbial 'beast mode.' Maybe a few too many. But more data is good data! And everyone was so *eager* when I asked. Anyway, I've finally hit a point where I can run a full alpha test, but that means providing... well. A goal. A *target*. You get where I'm going with this, right?"

She smiles. It takes Act a minute to realize that he can *see* that smile. He can see. The headset is off. He had not noticed. Even now that he has, he feels he is on the cusp of forgetting again. Its absence barely registers, because it *feels* like it's still on. It feels like—

It feels—

There is a noise outside. Act starts, eyes blown as wide as a deer in headlights.

Lys hums, hands returning to her keyboard. "You might want to start running, now."

⸻◦⸻

Google News Update:

The science of neural coding: how programming the brain... (NBC News)
Go on the hunt with (and for!) friends using new VR... (The Nerd

Daily)

34 missing and twice as many assumed dead as unsolved serial...
(ABC News)

LYTTA Brand VR update test: ARTEMIS Expansion...
(YouTube)

Major Key Inspirations:
The Myths of Actaeon and Lyssa

vii. the magpie

1. For Sorrow

It is dizzying, the sky. The brightness of it. The blue. How infinite its vastness during clear afternoons, and yet—*and yet*—the woman knows it to be no more than a façade. Beautiful and diaphanous, and soon to be full of holes.

Of decay.

How long, she wonders, will it take her to decay?

Grasses whisper their guesses into her ear as she gazes up—up, up, up—imagining the way that darkness will soon corrode the color from the horizon. In her mind, she can already see it: the open wounds of a hundred-thousand burst pustules, their ichorous discharge tar-thick as it drains.

Septic, her mind provides. By God, she would have Heaven rot.

"Will you be dying, then?"

It should surprise her, the woman supposes, when the little bird speaks. That it does not is a testament to blood loss. Unperturbed, she watches the magpie hop the length of a low hanging bough, springtime's final vestiges trembling in Its wake.

As fragmented flowers slough away, they reveal the clustered green beads of tomorrow's apples.

"Your soul is very pretty, my lady," the bird coos, appraising the woman's broken figure. When It cants closer, she fancies she can see iterations of ancient massacres in the oil and fetid humors of Its eyes. "I'd say it has an opaline sparkle. Can't you see it? Oh, I can. It's right there—no, a bit higher. Yes, there."

Although she can no longer feel the fingers she drags across her cheek, the woman can yet see what clings to them. Glittering. Damp.

Oh.

On any other day, her huffed exhalation might have been a laugh.

"That's n-not my soul," she tells the bird, lips twitching in a failed attempt to smirk. "It's just... a tear."

"Can it not be both?"

The question is considered. The sun tilts west. The magpie refolds Its monochrome wings.

"I should like to have it, I think," It murmurs, inching farther down the branch. "Would you give it to me?"

Ostensibly, the woman ought to stiffen in horror at a question so blasphemous. But really, what would be the point? She is too weary for alarm, and stiffening will happen later. It will happen naturally, whether she likes it or not. For now, curiosity suffices. "Why would I do that?"

"Because I can make it worth your while," the pretty bird says, tempting, feathers and petals flurrying as It alights upon her shoulder. From the wrong side of black mirror eyes, *something* gazes out. "I see you, my lady. I see what you want. I see how much you want it. And in that want, I see an opportunity—one that will benefit us both."

"What... do you see?"

"Why, that you're terrified. Of course, you're terrified. Who wouldn't be? Is there anything worse than being forever alone?"

That she cannot think of an answer does not mean there isn't one. It only means that her higher order functions have begun to shut down, synapses sizzling out in mimicry of the sun. Her brain is an open wound. Her thoughts are a hundred-thousand burst pustules, their acrid discharge tar-thick as it drains. The façade of her skin is beautiful, and diaphanous, and soon to be full of holes.

"That's what death is, you know. Being forever alone. Why, even the worms abandon you, eventually."

Her vision is full of holes.

"But it needn't be that way, my lady. Let me help you. Let me help *us*."

Lips part around the hollowed hole of her mouth. Talons dig into her clavicle, stabilizing the bird as It pauses. As It leans, and listens, and leers.

"Oh, no," the magpie bows, deferential in the way that only the most impious can be. "Thank *you*. You shan't regret it."

Like the rotted sky, that remains to be seen. The woman waits, staring into the appalling blue until its many shades have putrefied.

Until she can no longer hear her newborn son's screams.

⸺◆⸺

2. For Joy

Nothing brings the boy greater joy than the arms that will one day kill him.

He wonders what that says about him.

"Why, that you see the silver lining, of course," the magpie answers, stroking his hair with tender talons. Even when the bird is not a bird, It keeps Its talons. They curl at the ends of Its fingertips, rather like regret in a decision's aftermath, and he relishes the prickling sensation that they leave beneath his scalp. "Not everyone is lucky enough to know their death. Or to accept it so maturely."

There is some truth to that. Halves of truths. Thirds or quarters.

But when he walks into the magpie's embrace, he does so whilst imagining Its hands around his throat. Its talons burrow deep into the peeling soft of raw esophageal muscle, splitting his larynx like a fruit. He pictures his tissues ripped, his trachea exposed, and weak geysers of blood trickling down his neck as rain does a stump in the forest.

It comforts him.

"You'll do it just like that, won't you?" he beseeches, looking up with eyes as bright and dewy as the moss that clings to the trees. Impassively, the magpie gazes back, Its own eyes reflecting the fate of all things green. "Won't you? Do you promise to kill me just like that? Like you did my mother?"

A single talon cuts too deep, leaving a thread-thin swipe of scarlet along the camber of his cheek.

"I see no reason why not."

3. For a Girl

She supposes she must have had a father.

At some point.

Probably.

But if so, she remembers not a thing about him. The coarseness of his beard, the shape of his hands, the length of his stride; all are questions without answers. All are mysteries she cannot solve.

These days, even her mother's face blurs in her memory, as things so often do when viewed from a distance. The first time the girl had noticed her mental pictures warping, she cried, too heartbroken to register the ripples that those tears made when falling into the pond. Too young yet to appreciate the irony.

"Like a page in a storybook," sympathized the magpie, roosting blithely on the little girl's shoulder. "You held it too tight and crumpled the illustration beyond repair."

"So, I should have just forgotten her?"

"I did not say that."

"Then what *are* you saying?"

"That you ought to have treated her memory with gentleness," the magpie lectures, emphatically butting Its head against her cheek. Saline gives a particular sheen to stygian feathers. "Tucked it away somewhere private and safe. Only taken it out sparingly. Handled it more reverently, as one might a precious heirloom."

"Is that not what *you* are?" the child counters, frowning as a much clearer image materializes at the forefront of her mind. Its edges are precise, its colors vivid. Rarely does she muse upon her introduction to the magpie, and so when she accesses thoughts of that day now, she finds them in pristine condition. Nearly untarnished. "An heirloom, I mean. You were gifted to me like one. I use you like one. Like a pretty accessory."

There is a clarity to the little bird's laughter that brings more than Its mirth into focus. "Oh," It giggles, "I am a bit more than that."

"How much more?"

"You'll see, my pet," the magpie promises. "Someday."

—◦—

4. For a Boy

"Did you kill my mother?"

"Yes."

He looks more surprised than he should for someone who had already guessed the truth. The bird—who is, at this moment, not a bird—arcs a doubtful brow.

"I guess. I rather expected you to lie about it," the boy confesses, sheepish. "I had a whole speech that I... did you *really* kill her?"

The impossible gravity of the conversation is both affirmed and rivaled by the magpie's collapsar eyes. "Yes," It says again, before returning Its scrutiny to the pot on the stove. Soup is boiling there, aromatic and hearty. The boy watches, wondering, as It sprinkles a liberal handful of cranberry flowers into the mix.

"Have you killed others?"

"Yes."

"Many others?"

"Many others."

"Will you kill me?" he probes, in tones that seek confirmation rather than express fear. His boldness has always been a source of great amusement; the magpie titters, using Its ladle to swat the hand that creeps toward their evening bread.

"Yes," It murmurs over his yelp. "I will, my pet."

Pouting, the child sticks stinging fingers into his mouth. More offended by present abuse than by his eventual murder, he demands, "Why?"

In the flickering of the stovetop's glow, the magpie smiles Its answer, the impossible angle made by Its lips evocative of arrows. It points to something. Points out something.

"Time for supper," his guardian announces. "Come. Eat with me."

Outside the kitchen window, a tiny tiding of birds begins to chitter.

⚬

5. For Silver

She spends the majority of the exchange tucked behind the magpie's legs, peeking out only to scrutinize the farmer, or to scowl at his livestock, or to press the velvet purse she had been so proud to carry into her guardian's palm.

Coin and leash are exchanged. The young girl accepts the length of rope with the same gravitas she had the purse, although she is warier of the lamb than she had been the silver.

"Off we go, then," the magpie tells the child, nodding Its gratitude once more to the farmer. The farmer bows in reciprocation. "That should be all we need from the market. Let us return home."

"All right," the girl quietly agrees. She is quiet by nature. A subdued, tiny thing: frail and shy and hesitant in all the ways that her father had been resilient and boisterous and loud. Less his daughter, the bird thinks, and more of a throwback.

Déjà vu, It has learned, is to be expected when dealing with human genetics.

And so the magpie braids the girl's long hair whenever It can, threading in sprays of apple blossom and marveling at the way flesh and floral translucence work to complement each other.

A honeybee bumbles behind them as they meander the dirt path home. There is a mild breeze, one that smells of ozone and loam, and the sky above is boundless in its gruesome blues.

"Maggie?"

"Yes?"

"What are we going to do with him?" the little girl asks, warily eyeing the lamb. Like most animals, he has taken an immediate shine to the child, nuzzling against her thigh whenever their pace allows. He nestles and bleats, sweetness incarnate. He adores her, oblivious to the fact that his affection does naught but cause further distress. "Is he to be our pet?"

It is a distress born from knowledge. She is already aware of her queries' answers.

"No," the magpie tells Its charge, scythe-sharp talons paring gossamer palls from the sunshine. It gestures as if tossing a veil. As if laying a shroud. "He is to be our food."

"Tonight's?"

"Not tonight's."

"When?"

"When the time is right, silly girl," the bird chuckles, plucking an underripe apple from the closest of the trees. It comes free with a ligneous, satisfying snap. A shower of withered petals snows down upon their crowns. Without breaking stride, the magpie passes the green fruit to Its charge, who in turn offers it to the lamb. "He is too young now. Too lean. It would be a waste to kill him right away. So instead, we shall raise him. We shall feed him and shelter him. We shall take the finest care of him. You may even love him if you feel so inclined. But that will not stop us from slaughtering him, will it? Just like the pig. Just like the chickens."

"Just like me." She traces the contours of the lamb's velvet ear, contemplating those blossoms that had tangled in his wool. A moue reshapes her features as she looks to her guardian and ponders, "Is that why you named me Mary?"

The magpie's lashes flutter, not unlike the plumage of a startled bird. "Pardon?"

"Like that rhyme," the child clarifies. "The one about the lamb."

"Ah." Understanding rushes through the wild that is the orchard, the branches' solemn nodding mimicking that of a transforming head. Leaves rustle; feathers rustle. A bird alights upon the young girl's shoulder, Its polished beak black with the gloss of old gore. "No, my dear.

"I named you for your great-great-grandmother."

6. For Gold

"You don't mind being used this way?"

"Should I?"

The young man considers the aftermath of evisceration, idly tilting his dagger's blade. Left, right. Back, fore. Reflections slide off its sawtooth edge as smoothly as rain, his features replaced with liquescent ease by those of another—a face that the bird has been picking meticulously clean.

Gouged eyes weep aqueous tears. A split-mouth screams soundless supplications. Like the start of a morbid fairy ring, rib-tips poke through the mire of the corpse's mutilated chest, those bits of sinew that connect the magpie to Its meal still fresh enough to drip blood.

He hums, moving to blot his weapon clean. "Well, I heard somewhere that members of the corvid family are all scavengers. Looking at it that way, this is actually kind of a blessing for you, don't you think?"

"A rational conclusion to draw."

"Yeah. Yeah, it is." Nonetheless, a scowl leaves his brow lined with wound-deep furrows. "I guess it's just... that I don't think of you as a magpie. Or any kind of bird, really. Not even when you're wearing *this* form."

"Oh?" Bemused, the bird tips Its head back, *back, back,* opening wide the pit of Its throat. There is a moment in which reality warps, and his mind bends. Its mouth appears to be larger than the entirety of Its avian body. "If not a magpie," says the magpie, wondering, "what *do* you think of me as?"

The young man chews on his scarred lips, unsure how he should reply. Uncertain *if* he should reply. There is to the magpie's eyes a wetness reminiscent of inkwells, and he thinks, first and unbidden, of pens. Then of those other, less poetic things that are mightier than swords.

"Well, what does it matter, either way?" he says, grunting and stuffing his slaughter-smeared rag into a pocket. "You are what you are. I am what I am. And together, we'll be what we'll be."

"Which is?"

"Rich, if I have my way." The man smirks, returning the dried dagger to its sheath. "Between the two of us, there's no hit that can't be handled. May as well take advantage of that, I figure."

He settles back, resting his weight on the palms of his hands, as the bird nudges Its way through exposed and sundry organs, talons rippling the coagulating fluids that have pooled in the basin of the cadaver's torso. There is something meditative about the way It rips free Its next chunk of meat, swallowing again with all Its previous uncanniness.

"What is that human expression?" the magpie asks then, glancing vaguely at the canopy above. The sky beyond those leaves is vertiginous in its hues. It shakes off the lacy cutouts of sunlight that had lain in ethereal drapes over Its wings before clarifying, "The one about apples and trees."

Its charge blinks but does not otherwise comment on the inquiry's abruptness. "That they don't fall far from one another."

"Indeed?" Pensive, the bird wriggles Its feet, worming toes further puncturing the veneer of ruined skin. The blue has fled this body's veins. The flesh beneath has turned to rot. "Well, if you say so."

7. For a Secret Never to be Told

She never expected to live this long.

But then, neither did she expect to die so soon.

"You need not worry, my dear," the magpie soothes, in a voice softer than Its touch and with a touch softer than Its down. These are the only things that do not register as agony to her senses. "Your babe merely slumbers. He is the epitome of health. I will raise him as my own, and he will want for nothing."

There is more comfort in that promise, more aid and relief, than in any of the bottles on her nightstand, any of the pills or the salts or the chemical solutions. The irony of her increasingly labored breathing notwithstanding, the woman sounds grateful when she speaks.

"Will he... know about me?" she rasps, the words as cotton-thick as grisly sheets. With human hands, her guardian smooths the bedspread's lay.

"I will tell him."

A tremulous nod has the magpie smearing what sweat It daubed from her brow. "Will you t-tell him... that you killed me?"

The bird's answer is comprised equally of laughter and lachrymose. "Ah, history and its cycles. It is your body that is betraying you, sweet, not me," It says, tucking a matted curl behind her ear. Hairline light clings to the blood on Its talons. "But, I will tell him thus, if that is what you wish."

For a time, the woman deliberates Its offer, sinking a bit deeper into her pillows. A little farther into the encroaching dark.

"Will you… tell *me* something?" she husks, lolling weakly in the magpie's direction. The prompting cock of Its head is unnervingly, if fittingly, birdlike. Its silhouette, cast in stark blacks against the far white wall, can only be described in similar terms.

She does not fight the lethargy that presses her eyes closed.

"When I was very small," the woman breathes, "I vividly remember putting a rock in my mouth. It was purple, such a pretty, putrid purple, and I loved it. I wanted to keep it, so… swallowing it just… seemed natural to me," she admits, the event and her recollection of it strung together by confusion woven from a blend of time and experience. Its ties to reality are tenuous, but so is every connection one makes to their own past.

And that tangle of threads leads back to the heart of everything.

"You saw, of course," she whispers, feeble fists folding around a feeling—a truth—that remains difficult to grasp. "I… was s-so mad at you. For… making me… spit it out…"

From Its seat beside the carnage-covered bed, the magpie frowns, the beak-straight lines of Its lips pulled dramatically downward.

"I do recall," It murmurs, faintly confused. "But if it is an apology you seek, I am afraid you will be disappointed. I am not sorry about my reaction. Eating that rock might've killed you."

The bird's expiring charge smiles, her hand's spasm dismissive. "No. I—What you are… about to do," she mouths, the correction slurring even as she tries to over-articulate, "Is this… how y-*you*… love?"

The magpie says nothing. In the guttering gloom, ebony hair gleams, nacreous as feathers. Its eyes are the black of a parchment paper that had been written upon, over and over, until Its innumerable stories became something singular, something indecipherable.

"It is time, my dear," It tells her in too many voices. With too many teeth. With too many vertebrae cracking as It leans slowly, elegantly closer.

<hr>

8. *For a Wish*

He counts the flock as they alight upon the front lawn, fourteen wings clapping with fantastic theatricality.

"Maggie, look! All seven are back today! What do people call such a group, again?" he asks, glancing from window to kitchen, from magpies to magpie.

His guardian hums, preparing apples for a pie. "A murder, darling."

"Why?"

"Because humans have a fondness for pretty names and superstition," It drawls, Its humored tones as sweet and dry as the sugar It pulls from the cupboard. A bag of flour slouches beside it, along with a container of salt, and the little boy turns this reply around in his head with the same dexterity he does the rolling pin pilfered off the counter.

In his grasp, the cylinder spins. There is the thought, if fleeting, of celestial cycles and rounds of song, and it is less dizziness than it is existential vertigo that sees the boy gesturing to the bird with the whirling pin.

"But Maggie, you are not human. And you call them a murder, too. Why?"

It mulls on Its response for a moment, paring from an apple a single, succulent strip of skin. The spiraling peel glistens in the golden glow of afternoon, the same crimson as a grin.

"Because," It finally says, "*I* have a fondness for pretty names and accuracy."

<hr>

9. For a Kiss

"Daddy would kiss me goodnight. To scare away the bedtime monsters. Before he died."

"Yes, he would."

"Mummy would, too."

"I remember."

"You remember?"

"I do," It assures, tightening Its hold on her tiny, battered hand. "I was the wee bird in the cage. The one that your Daddy arranged beside your vanity."

The small girl blinks through this realization, her wide eyes puffy with bruises. Most of her body is puffy with bruises. In the accident's aftermath, she is dressed half in bandages, half in funerary attire. But for now, there is no one around to judge.

A light rain dribbles over the plastic of her umbrella, the erratic drum of each droplet quietly punctuating the hush. Tombstones drip; willows weep. A flock of corvids caw, creating ill-omened halos above their heads as they endlessly, ominously loop.

With hesitancy and a blustering of mist, the child looks upon the specter who looms beside her and wonders, "Will you kiss me, too?"

A thumb brushes across the pulse point hidden in her stitched wrist.

"I will kiss you once," It tells her, not without sympathy. The orphan is very tired of sympathy. And yet, she has suffered enough of it in recent days to recognize the difference between what her relatives had shown, and what this strange new guardian now gifts.

Biting at the split of her lip sends an electric spasm of pain shuddering through her extremities. "Tonight?" the girl presses, in a voice—with a heart—that fluctuates between eagerness and mounting trepidation. "To scare away the bedtime monsters?"

"No." It shakes Its head with just enough force to dislodge the beading rain. One drop splatters against the child's umbrella. Another shatters like crystal upon the cobbles. A third traces the edge of the not-bird's cheekbone, leaving a ruddy trail in its wake.

Distantly, the child is reminded of blood and bonds of fate, and in being distracted by these faraway thoughts, nearly misses what is said directly into her ear: "Tonight, should you wish it, I will hug you."

She starts, startled. This is a start, and it is startling. A new beginning. The girl marvels at the idea, watching the mobile of magpies.

She also steps closer, tucking herself beneath the arm that wraps around her shoulder.

"What about the bedtime monsters?" she demands, unperturbed by the undulating, plumose shadows that now tickle her temple. That whorl and coil and twist; that squirm, unnoticed, beneath flesh that has already been so damaged. "Will you protect me?"

"Yes," It vows, sincere. "I will."

"How?"

"I will keep sentry."

"All night?"

"All night."

"Forever?"

"For as long as you live, dear heart."

"Okay," Its newest charge assents, finally satisfied. Then, as only a child can be, immediately dissatisfied again. "So... When will you kiss me?"

The magpie deliberates for a minute, Its feather-touch skimming the curve of a little chin. Tilts it up. Up, up, up.

"On that day you shed a tear for me," It promises. "On that day we become family."

Like the wheel of fortune, eight birds turn. The two below them turn, as well: back toward the main road, where vinery and moss-eaten angels denote the cemetery's exit.

It is the last that they speak of the matter for many, many years.

***

10. For a Bird You Must Not Miss

His mother had loved magpies.

Smart, she called them. *Social. They create big groups in the spring—gather together like a family. It's sweet. Almost human, really.*

Almost.

"Good morning," he greets the magpies, because it would be rude to do otherwise. Not bad luck, necessarily—he doesn't believe in that sort of folklore, not *really*—but old habits die hard, and his nanny had always encouraged politeness, even to birds.

Especially to birds.

"Hmm. That takes me back. I wonder how Maggie is doing," he says to himself, wistful, as a warm wind rustles through the orchard's latticework canopy. Set as they are against the sky's macabre blues, the apple blossoms' pearlescent petals are so white as to appear void. Like little holes in reality.

Maggie would have appreciated that dissonance. He wishes he could share it with her, but he has not seen or heard from his nanny in decades. Not since he turned eighteen.

Not since his mother passed.

Well, hopefully, Maggie is alive and happy, wherever she has gone.

"What does one call an assembly of you lot, anyway?" he asks the magpies, conversational, while meandering to the shed to collect his gardening tools. In a playful row, all ten hop along after. One even carries a sprig of flowers in its beak. "I checked the internet, you know, but it listed nothing definitive. Or I could find nothing definitive, anyway. A *parliament* is a popular choice, as is a *tiding* and a *mischief*. Some say a *murder*, too, apparently. Have you any preferences?"

With the shed's rusted lock in hand, the man pauses, smiling slightly, as if waiting for some kind of answer. And arguably, there *is* some kind of answer in the clan's cacophonous cackle.

There is some kind of answer in how they surround him.

And there is some kind of answer in the way they take off—flapping, screeching, soaring into the bruise-colored Heavens—black to blue to nothingness, never to be seen again.

Major Key Inspiration:
"One for Sorrow"

viii. siren song

In spring, my lips skim the blade of Ligeia's shoulder.

I drink in the salt—the sea and the sweat—my tongue tracing the scars that spill along her spine. Even now, decades later, those lines are foam white. They curl into spindrifts. And while, beneath my fingers, this marred skin is soft, I know that further below that deceptive surface waits an ever-churning darkness.

A different sort of underworld.

The tide pulls on her toes, shackles her shins. Millenniums grind the past to hourglass sand, time ebbing and flowing around us, and I kiss those old wounds again, teeth grazing the nacre-lumps of her vertebrae as through a saline sheen I taste memories of loss.

"I want to do something special for you," I whisper. The ocean roars, demanding attention, but not even its power can drown out the passion that pulses in my decision. "I want to give you a gift."

"A gift?" Ligeia's smile glimmers, lined in the same liquid electrum as the horizon. "Have you not already spoiled me enough today?"

The golden gorse crown that I wove into her hair shifts when she cocks her head, its floral clusters clinging with the tenacity of mussels. Of muscles.

I have been experimenting, these past few years.

Love in all seasons, I murmured whilst bestowing the diadem, and she trembled in response: small, tectonic emotions shifting inside her. I thought it beautiful how we bring out ourselves in the other.

I think the same thing now, feeling in my core the voracious, possessive pull of the deep when I say, "I could never spoil you enough."

"You could," she insists. "You will. At this rate, I fear you shall spoil me rotten."

"I know enough about rotted things to assure you that will never happen."

Ligeia laughs, then: a rush of amusement, effervescent as it washes over me. I would happily suffocate in its warm waves.

"Well, that much I cannot argue. And I do, most genuinely, appreciate the thought. But I mean it when I say that you needn't do anything for me," my beloved assures, pearly teeth flashing as she lay a palm atop my own.

The pale of that hand covers mine with the gentleness of snow. It is a comparison, a *reminder*, that only serves to spur me on. My love for her strains against the seed-husk of my heart, threatening to burst into bloom when she coos, "I would ask for nothing except your return to me."

Above us, the sun floats like a boat in the sky. We turn our faces towards it, rosy-cheeked and dewy, and I feel my conviction take root, determined to grow in the soil that serves as my soul.

Ligeia grounds me. And I, she once confessed, make her feel like she is flying.

She deserves everything that I can give.

"I will return to you. I will *always* return to you," I vow. In a tangle of sea and weeds we fall back, sink down, cushioned by the ruins of times gone by. "But Ligeia, I can do more than that."

I will do more than that.

Before hell rises to rip me from her arms once more, I swear that I will set her free.

⋯⋯◆⋯⋯

"He no longer breathes, you know. You shan't get much help from him."

Ligeia's teasing drifts across the beach, musical as a melody. The whole evening is a song: the percussionist rush of pebbles in brine, the polyphonic groan of sailors and shipwreck, the staccato grace of Ligeia's step when she dances across the dead. Her fingers skim her sarinda's strings in the way that sunshine glints off tidepools, and in the face of such refinement, I cannot but acknowledge that my own scrambling, hefting, and dragging must look comedic.

I harmonize with Ligeia's mirth. How can I do anything but? It was silly of me to try and hide my actions. The surprise, after all, is not in *what* I am doing, but in what the result shall *be*.

"There is no need to resign yourself to meat-scraps. One may yet reach our coast alive," Ligeia continues, giggles evaporating into the musky summer gloaming. "I will of course offer such a man to you, should you require him. I have already rendered from this sorry crew what sustenance I need."

The moon rises, gilding my lover's bare skin in mercury. Her hair is starlight; her eyes, the bioluminescent lures of deep-sea marine life. In the wake of the night's feast, their glow has grown radiant—blood-born and blood-fed—and she burns, my personal Polaris. I can hardly blame the sailors for following her voice, for dashing themselves against the rocks. Anything to be closer to her.

It is a sentiment with which I can empathize.

My nails dig another inch into sloughing skin.

"I have no use for those who are still of this world. Just those who are to be of this earth," I pant, tugging the corpse in my arms further inland. One of his legs, only ever tenuously attached, is lost in my efforts. A splash of gore adds richer colors to the twilit shore. "For the task that I envision, his help shall be invaluable."

"Is that so?" Ligeia's gaze is ethereal in the crushing black. I resist the urge to swim to her, to press myself into her mouth. "His alone?"

"What do you mean?"

"I mean," Ligeia hums, "that the night is young, the ships are plentiful, and the earth here especially sandy. If you are looking to make loam, my love, you may yet need a hand." A pause. A smirk, curved as a wave. "Among other sundry parts."

The spume between her teeth is now a macabre, coral pink. Gods above and below, I can abstain no longer. Dropping the doomed deckhand at the bottom of a dune, I all but fly across the beach, eager to lick the horror from her serrated smile.

It is his decay that I need. Let him fester a while.

"What if I were to die?" she asks, the sea slipping from her skin in a sheet of liquescent diamonds. "What if, one day, I were to drown?

The waters recede further, leaving Ligeia naked from the waist down. The hips down. The knees down.

Down, down, down.

Staring at the swooping gulls, she presses, "What if one of the sailors survive and attack me? What if I slip and hit my head on the shale? What would you do if I jumped from one of the cliffs?"

They are terrible questions. I consider the dust between my toes, the dirt on my fingers. The sand that clumps around the coagulated remains of our slaughters, trying to conceal the truth beneath history, and abandoned shells, and the broken shards of lost riches.

"I suppose," I say at length, "that I would never return here again."

There is always something beneath the waves.

Life, of course. To a certain depth. And below that, death waits. But what comes after death? What lies under the underworld?

I can answer that.

Rocks. Stone. Sand. Earth. The ocean may plunge to incomprehensible fathoms, but it is earth that holds those waters. It is earth that supports them in the pitch and the gloom.

There is, I have learned, nothing so terrifyingly deep as the earth.

"But the *sky*," Ligeia sighs, sunbeams reflecting off her sea glass eyes. "Between the firmament and space, there is *more* of it than there is ocean. The sky is, well. I suppose we wouldn't say *deeper*, though I don't understand why. It's all water up there, too. Until it isn't. Much like the ocean."

"You would know better than me, beloved," I hum, inspecting the first of my summertime sprouts. Even as we speak, the seedlings' supple leaves are mining themselves from the mire, gleaming in gem-bright shades of bile. "But I would imagine that, if you can plummet through each, *deep* is a fine enough word to use. I shan't correct you, anyway."

Appreciation shimmers in the corners of Ligeia's smile. It is almost enough to outshine the sadness.

On the opposite side of the beach, the tide climbs higher. The shallows grow deeper.

"The ocean is all well and good," Ligeia continues, wistful. "It could absolutely be worse. I ought to be grateful. I usually am. Did you know, if I look long enough, I can sometimes convince myself that it's the same blue. But..."

"But that is only sometimes." There is to Ligeia's softness the lingering transience of seafoam. "Yes."

"I understand," I tell her. And I do. To push one's feet into fresh, fragrant mulch is nothing like the cold-hot descent into the Pit, though both involve being buried. "We make the best of what we have for as long as we have it."

"We focus on the gain," she agrees. "Not the loss."

"Not the loss."

Sunlight turns scars to lines of white gold. She hums an unfamiliar ballad. I turn my focus inward, downward, towards the thought of new plants, commanding willed seeds to germinate in their copper-scented fertilizer.

Then I watch those sprouts claw free from luxurious filth.

⋅◈⋅

I can hear it.

Below, beneath, beyond. It resonates through the earth—a promise made in the space where a hundred million voices should be. Roots wither in that silence. The breeze smells of asphodel.

It is coming.

⋅◈⋅

From carnage we come, and to carnage we shall return. Till then, we consume that which will consume us.

That is the way of life.

But there is a beautiful, untouchable pristineness to those who live like flowers do, dancing in the breeze while the horrors and humors they feed on slide cleanly off their bodies. Like rain from a petal, like grime from a leaf. Perhaps that is one of the reasons I so love Ligeia.

Perhaps. But if so, it is one of the lesser reasons.

"Will you not join me tonight?" Ligeia shouts, poised upon the singing shore. The sarinda twangs in her hands, and my whole heart yearns to be part of her symphony. "The moon is full, the waters warm, and the men full of delicious hubris."

In answer, I shove my toes into the soil. It helps to remind me of my plan.

"I will watch from here," I call from my budding plot. "Bring me blood."

There is a boat on the horizon, held in equal parts by sea and sky. But as the last of the sunset wanes, its smelt extinguished by the waters, that little vessel appears to float freely within an endless abyss.

Tonight is midsummer. It shall only get darker from here.

⋅◦⋅

"Love in all seasons," Ligeia recites, gesturing towards the spiny spirals of gorse. Their evergreen needles tangle as kelp does beneath bundled yellow ships. "I remember that one."

The pride in this pronouncement seeds my smile with dimples. "Do you recall any others?"

"Hmm." With due solemnity, Ligeia paces around my garden, squinting at what blossoms. Fractal bursts of herbs and flowers have imbued the once dull land with complex patterns: natural alchemic sigils that speak of life purchased with death.

It is a deal with which I am familiar. A contract that I know well.

As the ocean chants in the distance, Ligeia points again.

"Wormwood, yes?" she guesses. "That means *absence*. Or, sometimes, *do not be discouraged*."

In the wake of her wandering, the enchanted verdure waves. Thorns, branches, brambles, leaves. The green undulates to the rhythm of the turning world, the wheeling seasons, the ever-shifting tides. I nod towards one of the plants most desperate for her attention, its petals wriggling like the arms of a starfish. "What about the lemon tree?"

"What part of it?" she counters, proud of herself for catching my trick. "The leaves mean *everlasting love*, and the flowers, *fidelity in love*."

"And the stock?"

"Let me see..." She considers the row of botanical spires, admiring their architecture as she would that of a reef. Or, maybe, as she once did the steeples of coastal churches, their apexes covered in the eviscerated wet of the clouds. "*Bonds of affection*, yes? Occasionally, *promptness*. And the idea that *you'll always be beautiful to me*."

"Very impressive. The forsythia?"

"*Anticipation*."

"The maidenhair fern?"

"*Secret bonds of love*."

"How about the ipomoea?" I challenge. Beside me, the morning glory's precocious vines twine more tightly around their makeshift trellis. At first, I thought they had found themselves a pale rock but realized my mistake when the first of the tendril's ether-colored trumpets unfurled within the skull's socket. "What of them? I'm sure I've told you before."

The morning glory watches as Ligeia frowns, condensation adding an ommatidial glitter to its blooms. "Something about clinging?"

"*Attachment.*"

"Dammit." Ligeia's pout is fierce and immediate. Tracing the contours of a camellia, she sulks, "I was close."

You are adorable, the white flower wordlessly retorts. *Yours is perfected loveliness.*

It is a sentiment with which my whole heart agrees. I consider voicing it. But in the end, I extend my arms and ask:

"Would you like to be closer?"

⁂

I can hear it in the earth.

Below, beneath, beyond. In the ice-sharp darkness that cradles the whole of existence, that holds humanity within stalactite ribs. The throb of it resonates—like water, like blood—and I wish I could pretend that it does not sing to me, as seducing as if strummed on a sarinda.

There is nothing that can stop it.

There is no point in resisting it.

There can be no life without it.

It is nearly here.

On the day the sweet peas open, I know that it is time.

"Sit with me?" I ask, patting the ground. Try as I might, I cannot stop myself from sensing the vibrations of that gesture. From feeling the way it echoes, down, down, down through the roots, hollow and sonorous when it resonates between earth's vertebrae.

Like someone knocking on a door.

Sweeping loose hair over her shoulder, Ligeia perches herself between my legs. Tilts her head, offers her throat. Waits, expectant, for a kiss.

And oh, by the gods above, I love her. By the goddesses below, I love her. I love her, I love her, I love her. How can I do anything but offer her everything I have, everything I am, everything that is within my power to give?

"I have a gift for you," I breathe against her nape. My teeth skim her pulse, and I delight in watching her cheeks flush the pink of an autumnal sunset. "To help you pass the time while we're apart."

Intrigue ripples across her face. "I told you that you needn't—"

"I wanted to," I interrupt. Underneath my palm, branching scars shift, malleable as moonlight atop churned waters. There is so much of her that I would try to hold within cupped hands. But no—I couldn't. I can't. Not when I feel again the mutilated nub of a long-snapped bone: the vestiges of what had once been connected to her scapular. "I *want* to. Please, Ligeia, let me."

We are all of us carnage. Her old injuries push against my fingers, reminding me of seedlings trying to sprout.

"All right."

Nothing comes more naturally than helping them along.

⸺ ⸱❦⸱ ⸺

The pain *blossoms*.

Bud-bursts of agony follow her spine, wild and weedy and white. I sense diaphanous flowers, opening to expose nerve endings; I feel invisible roots, braiding and burrowing below.

Below.

Below, beneath, beyond. I follow the sensation as it travels, straining as rhizomes do, moving like water. Its flow is that of the damned: of the spirits whose suffering I shape, but do not own.

I have never owned the plants. I have never owned the souls within them.

I have never *owned* Ligeia.

She even screams like a song.

⸺ ⸱❦⸱ ⸺

There is an oceanic elegance to the cedar that splits Ligeia's shoulders in a pair of cresting waves.

I will be thought of, I know. She will think of me whenever she moves these ligneous bones. Whenever she spreads these verdant wings. Through them, she will *live*, and she will live for me.

"Well?" I murmur, sweet against her sodden brow. Dry against the damp of her. Fingers combing through her hair, as wild as Elysian fields, I ask, "How do they feel, beloved?"

Novelty has reduced Ligeia to a fledgling once more. There are minutes of struggle. One or two of concern. Patient, I watch as she stretches, then flexes, her every movement experimental.

Careful. So careful.

She need not be so careful. Venous vines of morning glory hold true where they twine around the wings' wooden framework, twilled together with arterial moonflowers. By their power, her plumage stays attached: feathers fashioned from maidenhair and forsythia, camellia and wormwood. Stock is taken of the stock, which flourishes as her alula, while gloss-covered lemon leaves prove themselves to be exquisite coverts, their blossoms shed in place of down.

Down, down, down.

Primary petals rasp together, arbutus, carnations, violets, and zinnias telling their secrets to the breezes that rustle through them: *thee only do I love; divine love; I will always be true; daily remembrance.* Yellow lilies and white hyacinth remiges flutter in kind, sighing promises about air, about prayers.

Ligeia swallows a breath as she might a mouthful of water.

Then, finally, she manages:

"They feel... natural."

⸺⦿⸺

Before I return to hell, we watch the solstice sunset drown itself.

Down it goes, down, down, down, displacing the darkness that had before been contained by the sea. Pitch floods the world, tidal as anything, and if I were a benevolent creature, I would wish for the sun to lift back into the heavens. I would want it to dry these saturated lands. I would beg it to bless the people with its light.

I am many things. I am not, however, that kind. Instead, I desire to see that golden chariot sink further. Deeper. To impossible depths, then below them. If I could demand it, I would have the sun descend beyond even the most distant shipwrecks, the most horrifying beasts. I would shove it into the earth as others might a pip. By my power, its luminance would be waiting for me when I finally arrived in my husband's domain: a warm friend in a cold place.

But that is a futile thought. Then it is a lonely one, as again it dawns on me that I will not be seeing the sky for many months.

"I'll miss it," I confess to both the shadows and Ligeia. Each cling to me. Each has claim on me. "I'll miss it terribly, even though I know that I'll see it again."

"Like me."

"Yes. Like you."

There is a gravity to Ligeia's nod, a weight that pulls on her chin, her mouth, her eyes, until we are both gazing over the waiting ledge of the Pit. It plunges like my hopes. For while I knew that this moment would be difficult regardless, I'd had faith that my gift would lessen my love's sorrows, and by proxy my own.

But no. Her heart is heavier than it has ever been, never mind the shed petals that lie shriveled in the gravel.

"It's time."

"It is."

"You'll need to let go," I remind, giving our hands a gentle tug. The motion eddies stagnant air, and between the sea-song and the death knell I catch aromatic notes of gorse. I bite my lip. "Ligeia, please. I have to leave."

"I know you do," she says, leading us nearer. Guiding us closer, until the black of the Pit pulls on her toes, shackles her shins. My feet grind dirt and dropped twigs to hourglass sand, time ebbing and flowing around us, around the ocean, around the entrance to a different sort of underworld.

Her grip does not loosen. If anything, it tightens.

I cannot stall any longer. "Ligeia—"

"Goodbye, Kore," Ligeia smiles, spreading wide her wilting wings. "We'll be together again soon."

And off the cliff we soar.

Major Key Inspirations:
Kore and Ligeia

ix. corpse road

It is a Tuesday, early, and the world outside Cyparissus's window is pearlescent with the promise of rain.

Nothing about this is remarkable. Nothing about it is worrying or sad. If anything, it is lovely. The weather, their plans, their mood. All lovely. They are surrounded by lovely people, in lovely Hyperborea, and everything about their life is lovely, just as it has always been. Just as it would, presumably, always be.

For all intents and purposes, Cyparissus is content.

But after a quarter of an hour examining the day's capsule—gel-filled and mint green, minutely stamped with the words MEMENTO VIVERE in restorative block text—they tuck the pill back into its recyclable distribution cup and return it to the kitchen's pneumatic tube.

"No," they decide. "Thank you."

When the light blinks red, they chuckle.

—◆—

Hyperborea's therapists are the country's pride and joy.

Decades are dedicated to training those who pursue the vocation, their efforts supported by funding, resources, and genuine public respect. It is a passionate lot who staff the therapy centers, and the results of their work stand as testament to this.

Similar things can be said of Hyperborea's psychologists. And its psychiatrists. Its general practitioners, too, although after Cyparissus's sessions with the aforementioned therapists, psychologists, and psychiatrists, the appointment with the GP feels a touch gratuitous. Beyond a papercut suffered while filling out forms, they are in perfect health.

Of course they are. Had there been the smallest scrap of evidence to suggest that Cyparissus's amygdala was more or less active than ideal, those symptoms would have been noticed long before now.

A requirement is a requirement, Cyparissus's cranial implant rouses to remind them. In its usual polite voice, the device asserts, *The importance of confirming one's condition in these sorts of cases cannot be overstated.*

Fair enough. Besides, Cyparissus figures, if the only news these professionals have to offer is *no* news, then there is nothing to make them change their mind. In fact, Cyparissus finds a sort of relief in the verification that their family history is spotless, that their bloodwork is clean, and that in the hundred years since their last full exam, they have developed no tells of disease, mental or physical or underlying or chronic or secret or otherwise.

Nothing is wrong. Nothing is malfunctioning. There is nothing that needs to be fixed.

Only after this has been established beyond dispute is Cyparissus given leave to visit the surgeon.

—◦—

The world is again pearlescent when Cyparissus is released from the hospital.

Another lovely sunrise. Another lovely day. As lovely as it ever is in Hyperborea, if not a little lovelier. *Much* lovelier, even. Has it always been *this* lovely outside? The dawn *this* lustrous? The colors *this* intense?

No, Cyparissus realizes. *But also, yes.*

The sky is the sky. It changes daily, as is the way of natural things. This feeling isn't about that. Not exactly.

Metaphor, their implant whispers, and Cyparissus nods in vague acknowledgement. They turn the idea idly in their head, noticing what light its edges catch before setting that truth gently aside. For now, anyway.

Some things are more transient than others.

And so, with the whole of their attention, Cyparissus celebrates the morning: cataloguing every nacreous shade that alchemizes the clouds as they are driven to the Lychgate.

In their arms, a blue glass lantern's weight grows steadily familiar.

—◦—

They have not had to shoulder a satchel since their schooldays.

The nostalgia evoked by doing so now adds an unexpected weight to the bag. They stumble briefly, looking for something to grab onto, before taking hold of a thought. A memory. Rose-tinted but thornless, and topical in a way that neural associations only sometimes choose to be.

Cyparissus remembers seeing a map of Hyperborea in their youth. Vividly cadastral, its projection onto the gymnasium floor playing an integral role in some grade-level activity they now recall in bits and dredged-up details. The rest is dust, sifting through their figurative hands.

Our objective here is killing curiosity, their teacher had decreed, fiddling with a wireless control panel. *In circumstances like these, there is no more effective a tool than fact. We want you to know what waits out there, my dears. It is not meant to be a secret. Let me repeat that. It is no secret at all.*

Due to the inherent restrictions of physics, that map had not been true to size. Obviously. And while Cyparissus is certain that, for educational purposes, their class was told its operational scale, that information was either forgotten or deleted centuries ago; these days, Cyparissus knows only that the dimensions of the holograms appeared proportionally correct when compared.

Precision does not matter to a nine-year-old. Nor to a nine-year-old's classmates. Not when presented with a menagerie of computer-generated buildings that they can pretend to smash.

See, children? Over to the west, that clean cluster of skyscrapers? Yes, where Dabria is tromping. That is the medical district. A show of hands, please. How many of you took a capsule today?

Good! Yes, that is the place where our prescriptions are created, and from where they are sent! Does anyone remember our unit about "illness?"

Oh, I agree, Thana, illness is scary. That is why we should be grateful for our medical district! Hm? Ah, yes, they are the ones who designed the capsules to taste like honey, Mritunjoy. An excellent question!

In the archive of their mind, Cyparissus's teacher speaks in the same clear, crisp voice as their implant. This is not accurate. But then, given the age of the memory, neither is it surprising.

And on the opposite side of Hyperborea, those sleek, imposing towers? What are—that's right, those mark the fringes of the technology quarter. Yes, Amara, we know that your parents work there.

Now, let's look towards the city center. Can you find the Obelisk? It sits like a pivot between important points. Precisely, good, there it is, near the Fountain of Fire. The Obelisk is a monument to those people who came before us, who were not fortunate enough to be blessed with the same opportunities that we are.

You five over there, I see what you're doing. Please show respect to our institution. Yes, that includes the simulation *of our institution.*

Blithely, Cyparissus wonders if they had been party to those mischievous attempts to decimate the cybernetic schoolhouse. If so, the incident is not amongst the mental recordings that have survived to adulthood. What they have retained instead, with an almost crystalline clarity, is the impression of Hyperborea's gordian sprawl twined around their feet: chrome spires and wire-lace networks, crocheted into a spiraling hub of human activity.

The middle of a spider's web is also called a hub, their cranial implant informs, just as it had when a smaller, more spirited Cyparissus loomed like a god over the hundred-thousand radial roads that the map showed unfurling from Hyperborea's forever-heart, past the outskirts and the boundary walls before fading into oblivion. *These silken nets are used to catch animals, protect offspring, and ensnare prey.*

There is no mention of *metaphor* this time, despite Cyparissus's belief that the word is apposite. Odd, that. Why not? Is it a glitch? A sign?

Unperturbed, they speculate how much longer they have until the implant ceases to function entirely.

⸺◆⸺

Unlike the highways and walkways and freeways that weave Hyperborea into a cohesive whole, the roads that extend beyond the Lychgate are unpaved.

No cobbles, only pebbles. No concrete, only dirt. No planned paths, only desire lines, forged by the feet of hundreds of thousands of likeminded strangers.

There is a charm to these roads, worn as they are directly into the earth. They are as well-trod as any metropolitan thoroughfare, and as well-loved despite lack of maintenance. They are as straight as Hyperborea's are twisted, as narrow as Hyperborea's are wide, and extend out endlessly, unspooling and dividing the leas beyond civilization's brink into wild, verdant segments.

HC SVNT DRACONES, Cyparissus's implant chirps. It is a thought recommended after running numerous algorithms, after processing the influx in related impressions and considering predictive data. *An anachronism. Used to reference the monsters sometimes added to areas of medieval maps about which nothing was known.*

"Now *that's* a metaphor," Cyparissus smirks. Their lantern, assigned with a splintered pane, spills its ethereal glow over the ground. Held high, it illumes everything that lies ahead. And yet, Cyparissus does not know what is coming. They know *nothing*.

They had almost forgotten what excitement feels like.

⸺◆⸺

Cyparissus knows it is bad luck to remain within sight of Hyperborea.

They are unsure *how* they know.

Internet rumors? Gossip, perhaps? Assumptions based on the plans shared by those who had taken this journey before them? Everyone is acquainted with someone whose friend has a friend who decided to leave; the superstition might have come from there.

Or maybe it was learned in the more traditional sense. Hyperboreans are human, even now—not birds in a gilded cage.

They were shown the exit young. They were told how to use it.

Do you see that singular door, my dears, built into Hyperborea's outermost wall? That is the Lychgate. If, someday, you should no longer wish to live in Hyperborea, you will not be judged, but neither will you be able to return.

Outside the Lychgate, children, is nothing.

"*Nothing*," Cyparissus mumbles to themself, glancing back at the progress they have made. Hyperborea is hardly more than a sliver of static now, its contours made molten by the ichor that drips from the sunset. Each step forward sees its metropolitan mass reduced. There is less of it, then less. Then less. "*Meaning: of no value.* But if a person were to see significance or worth in a purported lack thereof, is it really *nothing*?"

They pause, waiting for an answer. It is a token gesture. The lack of offered insight is expected. Not because Cyparissus believes their rudimentary philosophical ponderings have managed to stump their implant, but because there are no cell towers beyond Hyperborea's outermost wall. Their signal has been rendered to something suitably ironic.

"Hey." In lieu of being able to see into their own brain, Cyparissus looks upward, snickering. "I've been meaning to ask but keep forgetting. So. While I'm thinking of it and still have time—what is the meaning of life?"

The implant says nothing.

While they laugh, Hyperborea fades as if into nonexistence.

— ◆ —

The lantern is the first thing that Cyparissus notices: cerulean, guttering, and dented atop its finial, its eeriness exacerbated by the shepherd's crook upon which it is hung. In the gloaming gloom, it seems to float, like a pulsing ball of foxfire.

The second thing that Cyparissus notices is the body haloed beneath it.

"Hello," that body says, with the lackadaisical energy of a person going to sleep. "Well met, I suppose. But this is… this is my section of road."

"Don't worry. I won't use it," Cyparissus assures, bowing their head to acknowledge xir claim. "I'm tired, but I've still got a bit left in me." This is true. Or true enough. Even so, they hesitate at the expression they glimpse on xir face. "Would you mind, though, if I were to sit with you for a while?"

"Oh." The sentiment behind xir gentle frown transforms as xir attention slides back down the embankment, taking in the state of xir own limbs. Reclined like this, the slope has made odd angles out of everything: xir legs, xir neck, xir bent elbows. A summer breeze exacerbates the ruined geometry of xir hair. "If… you wish."

"Thank you." Cyparissus cradles their own lantern as they sink to the ground, the mechanism's intricate frame braced first against their chest, then their thighs. Finally, carefully, it is set in their lap, and they settle upon that liminal line where gravel becomes gorse. Where dimness becomes darkness and darkness becomes night, and night becomes something purer than Cyparissus has ever before experienced. "It's a very, uh. Pitch-black stretch that you've found for yourself."

Were it not for the combined strength of their lanterns, Cyparissus would not have been able to see the twitch of xir lips, never mind the softening of xir eyes.

"All of the stretches are nice, in their own way."

"Yeah?"

"Mhm. It just depends on how you *look* at them."

"I see." Hearing the unspoken prompt, Cyparissus tilts their chin in imitation of xir. Doing so makes them aware of the dew.

It glitters, constellatory. It reflects the galactic spill above—hazy teal and nebulous indigo, spangled through with snowy-white—to such a degree that their bodies appear suspended between mirrored heavens. Or they would, could they be seen from the neck down. As it is, the two appear to have become one with the abyss.

Cyparissus inhales, the perfume of geosmin pervading their lungs.

"In that case," they say, "why here?"

"Why not here?" xe counters, xir pupils collapsar-wide. "I could have walked farther. I could have stopped earlier. Would it have changed the stars? No. What matters is that I stopped at all. Couldn't really admire them properly, otherwise."

Their own eyes dyed by astral, Cyparissus hums in understanding.

"Hyperborea had highways and walkways and freeways," they comment, craning their head back further. Further. "No Milky Way, though."

Xir exhale contains more agreement than breath. "Nothing like it, is there?"

"Nothing at all."

An hour later, a single star falls. Its light is not alone in winking out.

Cyparissus encounters others.

Bodies. Corpses. The two are not always initially synonymous, but they will become so soon. That much is inevitable when traversing these roads.

Dead man walking, Cyparissus's mind supplies in their own voice, watching someone else's lantern bob in the distance. They are uncertain who that wanderer is, or what brought them here, or where they will end up. *There is no certainty except in the lack thereof.*

It is then, in a visceral rush, that Cyparissus realizes how upsetting it can be to know only what one does *not* know. How wearisome it is, how limiting. There is a unique frustration in being forced to define a person, a place, or an idea not by *presence*, but by *absence*. By what may or may not be *lacking*. With naught but a feel for the hollow parts of a concept's shape, Cyparissus can appreciate why the indefinite was once anthropomorphized into something grotesque.

Monsters. Men. Metaphor, they muse, readjusting their grip on their lantern. *Does the overlap provided by my situation give credence to that trope about 'men being the monsters all along?'*

Maybe.

Their mouth still tastes like honey, sometimes.

"Mine too," Cyparissus is told by another traveler that afternoon. The two had stumbled upon each other beneath a copse of aspen trees, having been similarly mesmerized by the canopy's undulations.

"It's like the leaves are swimming," ze had said in lieu of a greeting, and Cyparissus replied, "A million mercurial fish, flickering in the fathomless vast."

No doubt that is what had inspired their discussions about *school*. And from there, conversation flowed.

"I don't begrudge them for it," ze insists, though zer nose scrunches as ze says so. Cyparissus suspects the claim does not feel correctly formed in zer mouth, the words selected not-quite-right, but ze has to spit them out before trying again. "I mean, I'm thankful. I am. For all the capsules and pills and therapies and... everything. Medicine, technology. They are forces for good. Or, well, they *can* be. And for the most part, I think they have been. I do believe that everything was offered to us in good faith, anyway. With good intentions. I could compare Hyperborea to a parent, trying hard to shelter vir child... So hard, ve forgot the harm that denying a child pain will cause."

Their lanterns, though mismatched, smolder the same shade of cobalt. Cyparissus nods.

"The unknown is scary. Makes sense that people would want to be protected from it."

"Yeah, well. Just goes to show that nothing lasts forever. Not even fear." Ze grins: a wide, lopsided thing, full of froth-white teeth. Kaleidoscopic patterns ebb, sway, and swirl across zer face, inviting Cyparissus to reflect on morality.

They are in the process of doing so when ze clears zer throat with a giggle.

"Apropos of nothing," ze continues, "I get that we're all on solitary journeys. I mean, that's life. But just because they're *solitary*, doesn't mean they need to be *lonely*. Right?"

"Right."

Another quicksilver flash. A hand breaches the space between two bodies. The finger that loops around Cyparissus's pinkie is as thin as a line, hooking into their heart when ze murmurs, "Walk with me, please? Just for a while. Just until the next turn."

Cyparissus does.

<hr>

The next turn reveals a pond, rolling hills, and no lanterns besides their own.

"Perfect," ze decides, so Cyparissus helps retrieve from zer sack a collapsed shepherd's crook.

It is during the process of expanding the rod that they spot the corrosion. There is a missing peel of paint near its heel. Its absence exposed delicate metal to air and moisture, and now rust clings to wounded ornamentation like a scab.

When did that happen? Why? How? Tracing the obol of tarnish, Cyparissus mulls on the damage's implications in the same way they do their lantern's broken glass. *What could this tell us of its history?*

It is after glancing the edge of an eroded epiphany that they correct: *No. What stories?*

History, after all, is ongoing. Its reach extends in both directions. *Stories*, on the other hand, are finite. They have a beginning, a middle. An end.

They end.

"Exactly so," ze says, fiddling with zer lantern while Cyparissus talks through this insight. "Which is why I always got confused when people talked about the 'history of the cosmos.'"

"Ah." Cyparissus blinks. They pick off another grit-brown flake. "That's... well. You're not wrong. Someday, there *will* be nothing."

"I mean, yeah. Stay or go, there's no escaping that eventuality." Ze chortles, amiable as ever. "But you know, there was nothing *before*, too. And that worked out all right, didn't it?"

For a full minute, Cyparissus does not reply, focus drifting to the road that lies behind them. A road that fades into oblivion, its reach extending in both directions. A road that led them here.

"I suppose it did."

⸺ ⬦ ⸺

Zer preparations are nearing completion when eventide rises, rolling between the knolls on waves of sapphire and azure. Eventually, inexorably, the current grows deeper, navy crests crowned by spumes of shimmering mist. It grants a luminosity to the terrain, even as the ground is flooded by shadow.

Damp weeds ripple, cold where sprays meet skin. Cyparissus's lantern is a comfortable weight in their lap, its heat just on the right side of too warm. Zer lantern shines above zer, spectral.

"Hey. Can I... ask a question?"

"Sure."

Lain in a pool of cobalt light, ze turns zer head to Cyparissus. "What made *you* choose to leave?"

When Cyparissus leans back, there is an instant—ephemeral but acute—in which they want to compare condensation to tears. But they do not. Instead, they think about mercurial fish, and the togetherness of shoals, and water memory, and the oceanic pressure of the emotions behind their breastbone.

"Nothing," they say.

Neither says anything more.

In the morning, dawn breaks in shades of opalescent pink.

Time shifts the world as a child would an abalone shell, and the sky shifts in kind: mauve to red to iridescent blue. Seafoam clouds are already gathering on the horizon, dribbling gold and leaking streamers of cerise; the sun hoists itself high on those chatoyant rays, and both parties decide to move on.

Only Cyparissus stands to do so.

Cyparissus has a few days' worth of water left in their canteen when the road ambles past a meadow.

There is nothing special about it. Just tall, supple grasses threaded through with crawling vines, green on green on green on green until they reach the robin's egg horizon. Their snarl reminds Cyparissus vaguely of a nest, and the many ways in which a nest and a web are similar. Those other ways in which they are different. And how both can feel impossible to leave, even when it is imperative that one do so.

"Nothing for it," they joke to themselves, jamming their shepherd's crook into the earth. That the roadside slants means that their crook does, too: the shaft bowing forward in homage to archaic cemetery angels. The lantern itself hangs with the solemnity of a head.

There is a moment, once everything has been hooked into place, when Cyparissus's arms are too light, their hands too empty. They touch their chest as they gaze into the chamber's throbbing core, feeling as they do a surge of giddiness. They delight in this feat that they are about to see to *completion*.

It has been so long. They have carried it so far.

"Thank you," they tell what beats beyond the glass. "I did nothing exciting, nothing important, nothing that will be remembered beyond a generation… and that was *everything*."

The fractured pane turns to prisms the lantern's uncanny gleam. Cyparissus lowers themself within its nimbus, hands folded atop their chest. The cord that wends between them—plugged from bone to lantern base and nearly forgotten until now—slips like silk between their fingers.

More metaphor.

Though, in fairness, that seems appropriate.

⸻◆⸻

Day is transitory.

So is twilight.

So is the universe and nature and all things terrible and beautiful. In the tangled sward before them, an orchestral ramble of ipomoea tune their trumpets to the moonrise. It is a production that the flowers pace to the metronome flashing of fireflies.

Light, then dark. Here, then gone. Something, then nothing.

Serenely, sweetly, the serenading symphony silently swells. It is an overture as much as an epilogue; it is a chapter, self-contained and analogous. It is a story, in its way. And it will do as all stories do.

Cyparissus, smiling, gives a pull and does the same.

Major Key Inspirations:
Cyparissus and Hyperborea

x. unfair grounds

I. Parsley

In Scarborough, parsley grows in abundance.

These are the arid lands, otherwise. Sun-blistered, desert red. They are perfect for seedlings that must smolder in nine separate circles before germination.

Perfect for them, and nothing else.

No one else.

"Please, no!"

Agony echoes from the bowels of the fairground's cooling pits, temporarily converted for the monthly town meeting. Careful families pick around each sudden drop, ignoring the screams as easily as they do the deconstruction of the PA system. Pairs fold excess burlap, their steps parodying a dance.

"Why—?" the chosen shriek, avian, over the sound of bulged eyes popping. Of steel chairs being carted, and nameless children laughing. Winds whisper answers through the trees' recycled aluminum leaves, their branches clawing caverns into the ash-eaten sky's topography. But still, crackling voices demand, *"Why?"*

Their confusion is understandable. It really is, given the presence of so much parsley.

ScarB-Cit #776 can empathize.

"I dreamed of this," ScarB-Cit #036 is saying, all thirteen years of his spry and wiry body enveloped in the lush of a luxuriant emerald patch. His lashes lower. His voice has lowered, too, recently, pulled down by gravity even as his limbs rebel, arms sprawling outward like roots, offshoots, vines. The dry brown of his flesh melds with the dry brown of the earth, and ScarB-Cit #776 imagines him dead: gnarled and knotty from dehydration, the leathery remains of his skin nibbled away by worms, sloughing into soil.

He will be so beautiful then.

He is so beautiful now.

"I dreamed of this," ScarB-Cit #036 says again, relaxing the creaking vertebrate of his spine. One by one, one by one. His neck shifts a fraction, serpentine in the greenery. The opalescent eyes that gaze up at ScarB-Cit #776 are the same bright white as the sun, and they imbue his skin with a similar warmth.

"When?" ScarB-Cit #776 asks. "When did you have this dream?"

"Last night. It was the most terrifying nightmare. Did you not have it, too? All I knew was that I needed parsley—desperately, desperately." A shudder, elastic features twisting. ScarB-Cit #036 inhales heat, deep and measured and languid; lips part, and ice escapes in glittering rings of smoke. "I had a window box, in my dream. As if the seeds were somehow sentient, they sprouted there. Suddenly. *Viciously*. They overtook everything. Before I could blink, my whole life was in strictures, consumed by a void of vegetation. I cut it all down. Or I tried to, anyway, but the sickle I'd found somehow wound up wedged in my heart. Maybe I swung it too hard."

When russet fingers twitch with thought, the sprigs braided between them grow.

ScarB-Cit #776 smiles, waving a palm over the bushel beside his own crossed legs. For him, the flora merely shivers. It is not surprising. Parsley grows for the wicked, and there is no one more wicked than ScarB-Cit #036.

ScarB-Cit #776 needs to keep practicing.

"What do you think it means, 7-7-6?"

In ScarB-Cit #776's lap, the ichor splattered parchment of *New World, New Order (Re)Educational Handbook: For Kids! Edition 4.295* flutters in an herbaceous breeze, as if some ethereal entity is thumbing through it. It pauses on a page with dog-eared corners, margins covered in the fibrous fungus indicative of a chapter on botany.

If this plant grows in your garden, the tenebrous ink warns, *you will be dead before the year is out. Bad luck, bad luck, bad luck.*

"Dunno."

Bad luck. But then, there is no other kind in this place, this village that eats its own citizens alive, squirming and garnished with parsley. ScarB-Cit #036 knows that. Everyone knows that. But denial is a survival technique so important that it is taught to the masses these days, not just government officials.

"Oh, c'mon." ScarB-Cit #036 rolls his eyes, then his body, flipping onto his stomach and resting his chin in his hands. His back is a mess of dirt, clinging clods and arthropods. His grin is that of a skeleton half-buried in its grave. "You're the best student in our class. You must have *some* idea."

ScarB-Cit #776 does. Like many before him, he has ideas and says nothing. His favorite idea is touching his friend's throat, dipping into the spongy warmth of his mouth and following ScarB-Cit #036's tongue down the tube of his esophagus, leisurely fingering every bump and ridge of muscle that he finds along the way. In his mind, he loses himself on that twilit trail, wandering until he is swallowed by a darkness as all-consuming as the heart of the Mayor (all hail, all praise).

Kissing would be less intimate, but he cannot picture that without blushing.

He stops picturing things all together.

"It's probably nothing," ScarB-Cit #776 assures instead, wiping mud from his companion's nose. Condensation dews wherever their skin meets, pearling in fat drops and falling like rain. The foliage below struggles beneath the weight of it all; ScarB-Cit #776 can empathize with its plight, too.

In the distance, through metallic trees, the living chant their village's ancient motto: *I will show you life in a handful of dust.*

—♦—

II. Sage

They stuff-stuff-stuff him full of sage, the plucked leaves rubbery and swollen like tongues. Pushing, intrusive, suggestive, unwelcome. His cheeks turn white against the bulge, flesh thinned by insisting fingers and formless mush.

ScarB-Cit #036 cries.

Raised veins rub against his soft palate, accompanied by thoughts of sandpaper. Dust. Handfuls of it. Stringy stems molest his uvula with feathery touches, slipping deeper and deeper. Further and farther.

He gags. With great heaves and guttural retches, ScarB-Cit #036 tries to force the mulched herbs out of his mouth, bracing himself on his knees as frantic, clawing fingers scrabble at the sigils carved into the floor.

His is an animalistic fear. Appropriately so, ScarB-Cit #776 muses, reminded as he is of scapegoats and sacrificial lambs.

"*Shhh. Shhh...*" Cooing, ScarB-Cit #776 rubs at ScarB-Cit #036's back, every inch the personification of detached comfort that the government has decreed he be. It had taken him some time, yes, to get used to his new skin, but ScarB-Cit #776 has since fit himself nicely into his predestined role. Now, it is ScarB-Cit #036's turn to do the same.

He must.

Everyone *must.*

"Swallow," ScarB-Cit #776 urges into an ear deafened by blood. He slips an arm around ScarB-Cit #036's thin waist, as tender as the sage itself, and nestles it into the fold between torso and pelvis.

Hips press into the camber of a quavering backside. Fingertips are replaced by lips. *Lips*, pale and segmented and moving, redolent of the maggots in ScarB-Cit #776's fantasies.

Oh. It is a tease more than a realization. Despite himself, ScarB-Cit #776 cannot resist nipping at ScarB-Cit #036's shoulder, paying tribute to the worms that have forever lost their claim to this exquisite, convulsing body.

It belongs to the village, now.

"Swallow," ScarB-Cit #776 murmurs again, front to back and holding him, so sweetly, so safely. "The previous Mayor—all hail, all praise—commanded that you do so. That was his final order. He didn't, so you have to. You have to eat it all."

Saliva slips in viscous tendrils, dribbling down his chin. Trembling tears follow in kind. With fingers curled around his gullet, ScarB-Cit #036 does as he is told, his Adam's apple bucking wildly against ScarB-Cit #776's palm.

The tantalizing drag of flesh on flesh sends static through ScarB-Cit #776's synapses, an anesthetic that numbs him to all other stimuli. Leaning in, he whispers meaningless, distracting trivia into ScarB-Cit #036's nape:

Sage is for wisdom, long life, good health. Sage cures skin sores, dyes hair silver.

That much is obvious. When he nestles closer, ScarB-Cit #776's blonde hair looks unnaturally bright against ScarB-Cit #036's newly grayed tresses. Those hoary strands shine with a winter frost's brightness, glinting in the piercing fluorescents of the council office.

They're known as healing plants in many cultures. Native Americans used them as a spiritual cleansing agent.

A gentle hand pumps the length of ScarB-Cit #036's throat. Its pair is splayed low across his belly, massaging ingested herbs into place. Knots appear, then settle within writhing bowels.

Done.

For now.

ScarB-Cit #776's embrace tightens a fraction, supporting his friend in place of joints and muscles. Air shrieks through gaps in spice-speckled teeth; croaks and coughs propel ScarB-Cit #036's body back into ScarB-Cit #776's. He looks like a corpse. And it's funny, almost, since ScarB-Cit #036—*this* ScarB-Cit #036—will never be one.

No. Sage creates life. Gives life. Gives immortality. And. And.

"Th-there's one… one more th-thing…" ScarB-Cit #036 rasps into ScarB-Cit #776's ear, the back of his snowy head connecting with a shoulder. His voice is wracked equally by pain and omniscience. Somewhere near the door, a councilor is thanking ScarB-Cit #776 for his assistance.

ScarB-Cit #776 is not listening. Not to his coworker. "One more thing?"

"That s… sage does…"

"Yes?" ScarB-Cit #776 prompts again, features open to show interest. Limbs closed to show possession.

With a ragdoll sag, the man in his arms relaxes coiled muscles. His head lolls, his features flip. Gravity tugs at his hair, just as the pearlescent gleam in his too-round eyes tug at ScarB-Cit #776's gut.

There is something off about it. Something both terrified and terrifying.

"0-3-6?"

A smile creeps over sallow features, glossy and winding and upside-down, so that its bow almost looks like a frown. The deepest, most dangerous frown, with a sickle-sharp arc. At this angle, the corner of ScarB-Cit #036's lips seem to pierce through his chest, and ScarB-Cit #776 feels oddly jealous. He longs for that mouth to cut his own into tatters.

"It increases... one's mental capacity," ScarB-Cit #036 confides. Giggles, even. Creamy liquid beads upon his lashes, draining from beneath translucent lids. Tears, but glutinous. They ooze, leaving streaks of calcium and chlorophyll.

ScarB-Cit #036 does not seem to notice. His focus is on the skulking ring of council members, watching as they slowly, slowly close in, moving like the curves of a pentagram drawn in tar. "I know. I know what happened. I know what *will* happen. To you. To Scarborough. I know *everything*. They made me know everything, and now they're going to take it away. They're going to kill me. Soon, I will be dead again."

The newest of the council members arches a brow. His is an ouroboros bemusement: it feeds on itself as the shadows edge nearer.

"They can't kill you," ScarB-Cit #776 retorts, the pendulum of his emotions swinging from exasperation to trepidation. Back and forth and back and forth. Like glances, like a rapport. Like secrets told and retold until they have become lies, and ScarB-Cit #776 is reminded of bedtime stories he was told as a child, fables from old cultures and even older religions.

ScarB-Cit #036's smile is a forbidden thing.

"They can't kill my body," he agrees, quiet. "But they can kill me."

ScarB-Cit #776 can do nothing but believe him.

Believe him, and hug tighter.

III. Rosemary

ScarB-Cit #776 tries not to think about that day.

He tries not to think about much, most days. Thinking is painful, dangerous. Generally inadvisable.

But the brain has a stem, and therefore roots, and those roots run deep. Tenacious, tangled weeds, intertwined and layered. Tortuous. Yet also stabilizing, forming meshwork in so much loose earth.

So.

He tries not to think, forgives himself when he does, then redirects his energy to trimming the philosophies that form flowers after feeding on the loam of his subconscious. It's tedious, but he does not want to destroy those kernels entirely.

Not *entirely*.

He has seen what happens to a mind uprooted.

There's rosemary, that's for remembrance. Pray you, love, remember, he silently quotes, focus drifting back. Shakespeare, eleventh grade English. The pungent, chlorinated odor of burnt ozone. ScarB-Cit #036 sitting behind him, listening, twiddling his voice-to-text recorder pen. Passing notes. Sharing glances. Their teacher, droning, *And there are pansies, that's for thoughts. And here, a bleeding rose, its sundry petals peeled back in flaps of dissected muscle, freeing the black widow hoard that have nested within and rotted its core.*

The core. The core of ScarB-Cit #036 has rotted, smothered and strangled by so much pruning and poison. The labyrinth of his brain, forcibly altered again and again, no longer bears much resemblance to the landscape that ScarB-Cit #776 had loved.

But still.

Still, beneath it all, beneath the ground, beneath blossoms of different colors and sizes, those roots are…

He shakes his head, rustling the musings that bud there. Clothes are rustling, too: a button-down and silk tie, the latter loose around his collar as ScarB-Cit #036 opens his front door.

"Hello?" he greets the corridor, frowning. The dank, ectoplasm-splattered halls of the mayoral apartment complex appear empty. They *should* appear empty. To the average person, they *would* appear empty. But ScarB-Cit #776, like all government officials, has learned to abuse his Power.

Suspicious, ScarB-Cit #036 glances to his left and right. Up and down. And there. His scowl deepens, adjusting cotton sleeves atop tattooed identification.

"Again?" he murmurs, crouching. With single-minded grace, he plucks the spray from his doorstep, examining it against the visible slats of the gunmetal sky. Its aroma teases, wafting like an aphrodisiac. ScarB-Cit #776 can smell it too, hidden as he is. See it when the sprig immediately withers.

"Hmm," the Mayor (all hail, all praise) hums, noncommittal, while watching the twig delicately implode, green to brittle gray. Left a shriveled sliver of its former self, its needles fall away like memories, land like gentle rain. They play chords upon concrete. Music, emptied of emotion. A funerary march.

The dead holds his posy, unaware that he is being honored.

"Poor thing," he mutters to no one, cradling the emaciated shoot in his palm. The most determined of the leaflets—clinging, stubborn, to its stem—brushes against ScarB-Cit #036's index. ScarB-Cit #776 is reminded of *New World, New Order (Re)Educational Handbook: For Kids! Edition 4.295.*

How long has it been since he last thought of that book? Last read it? Last *needed* to? ScarB-Cit #776 had it memorized, once upon a time; now, he can only recall bits. Page 485, which claimed that one could steal another's love by tapping their finger with rosemary. Page 610, which advised winding wreaths of the herb into a bride's hair. Page 929, which stated the plant should be used as a symbol of fidelity.

He does that, at least.

ScarB-Cit #036 slips back into the safety of his home, and ScarB-Cit #776 knows that there will never be anyone else.

<hr>

IV. Thyme

There is no thyme in Scarborough.

This is by council decree. *No thyme*, they insist, even as sprigs are sewn onto shirts and threaded through buttonholes. *No thyme,* because the protection it offers is ineffectual, just like guns or holy water or lawsuits filed by the poor. In another village; in another life; in another, parallel universe, the plant might have been used as a symbol of strength, or happiness, or courage, but not in Scarborough.

No, not here. Not now, where its existence is denied with as much vehemence as the politics and policies before The Great Burning. Thyme does little but trim shallow graves.

ScarB-Cit #776 is grateful that he chose to wear some today.

"I will show you life in a handful of dust."

There are too many people. ScarB-Cit #776 can tell as much from the fairgrounds. Elbow to elbow, hip to hip, the villagers shudder and sob and overheat, pyrotechnic growls growing louder in their ears. On a plinth above, numbered balls glisten in a tub, their non-plastic threatening to melt. The loudspeaker shines a starry silver, like the hair of the one stood behind it.

"ScarB-Cit #583, ScarB-Cit #192, and ScarB-Cit #309. Your food is ours. Your water is ours. Your air is ours. We will live because you will not."

The wailing begins. Unnamed youths screw their talons into the ankles of the ill-fated, fingers coiling like ivy and corroding bare skin.

"ScarB-Cit #008, ScarB-Cit #776, and ScarB-Cit #041. Your food is ours. Your water is ours. Your air is ours. We will live because you will not."

The young pull at their elders. They yank. The burlap surrounding converted cooling pits undulate like epiglottises, rolling and rippling as selected residents are dragged into that gaping abyss. Outcries are swallowed by the belch of shifting sediment, coal and tinder; grooves are dug into the earth by scrabbling, pleading hands. ScarB-Cit #776 falls, pawing at mirages, when five little nails hit bone.

White. Black. Colors. The latter flair behind his eyes, kaleidoscopic explosions of vein-violet and bruise-blue creating webs between the clouds of a pollution-smeared atmosphere. His knee has burst against a rock. Life forces ooze in trellis patterns, each droplet a spider scurrying from a split cocoon.

"Ah—!" ScarB-Cit #776 hisses, a fine mist of agony. His ears fill with the PA system's feedback static, fuzzy-gray and electric. And pulsing. And *spreading*. The current crackles through his extremities, contorting his muscles, paralyzing his throat.

And it's funny, isn't it, that he should only realize how much he wants to say—how much he should have said—when the moment is gone, his chances up in literal smoke.

"We will live because you will not."

Something thin and probing is slipping past his lips, branching outward, closing around his vocal cords. His thigh. Hooking through his upper right rib. He jams his eyes shut, focusing on childhood whims and daydreams and bright, happy moments, even as his whole body lurches.

ScarB-Cit #036.

Buttons plow trails into the dirt. Fingers snap beneath trampling feet. The thyme on his collar smells of rich, broken soil, as black and as cold as the voice in his head.

I know what will happen. To you, that voice promises, as if gifting ScarB-Cit #776 some secret salvation. Some consolation, some comfort. *I know everything.*

"We will live because you will not."

It is not enough.

It is *not enough.* It is never enough. It has never been enough, will never *be* enough. And it is not fair. *Not fair,* these destinies they have been given, this ruined earth they have inherited, the arbitrary end to which this all has come.

Why? *Why?* The ache of it makes him want to scream. To thrash, to curse and hurt and be hurt; to beat himself against the ground until he destroys his own nerve endings, loses all sensation. Until his outsides are as bloody and broken as his insides.

In lieu of that, ScarB-Cit #776 smiles, features contorted by a mouthful of invading parsley, of lingering regret. He convulses as flames lick at his shins. His knee vanishes beyond the burlap, and he thinks of parallels. His waist, and he humors an epiphany, too little, too late. His shoulders, and he recalls the words have existed for eons.

Remember me to one who lives there / He once was a—

"We will live because you will not."

It is dragged out for centuries. Or maybe it happens in an instant. There is no way to tell which.

There is no thyme in Scarborough.

Major Key Inspiration:
"Scarborough Fair"

xi. umibozu

"This is the part where you try to escape," It says.

"I think you are the reason I am here," I reply.

<hr>

The blackness weighs nothing. It weighs everything. It weighs upon my sanity more than It does my vessel, and there is something significant in that, I think, as I watch the creature peal Itself away from the horizon, featureless, oil-slick, and drooling. It wasn't, and then It was. It was, and now It is. It is...

It is dusk, but the red skies behind It offer no delight.

To be fair, there is nothing here to delight in.

I am dizzy. I am drenched. I am an ocean, self-contained. My blood rushes through me, a tidal force that rises and razes as brackish fluids dribble from my pores. Flying fish have eaten all the butterflies in my belly; now, my stomach flops. My extremities ache. And my thoughts, innumerable, bubble into effervescence, popping uselessly in the whirlpool between my ears. Panic smothers what breath I had managed to retain, leaving my lungs—like so much else—crushed and empty.

Inside, I am a storm.

Outside, the sea is tranquil.

I stare. It stares. We stare as It rises up, as It flows out, as It crests over the shifting, seraphinite surface from which It had so suddenly emerged, neither of us speaking when It pours Itself into the seat across from me. Spume has splattered in Its wake, foam dregs fizzling atop my toes. It molds Itself into a shadow, Its bulbous head a molten-tar facsimile of a man's.

"Hello," I hear myself croak.

"Give me a ladle," the creature greets in turn.

I cannot say this is what I expected.

My tiny boat wobbles in the encroaching twilight. I look to be alone in the waters. I wonder if I *am* alone, if I have lost my mind as well as my way, even as I gawp into a darkness far deeper than the void that looms above. Far colder than the abyss that waits below.

"Give me a ladle," It whispers again, a familiar, steady pulse to Its voice. Vowels and consonants tumble one over the other over the other when It speaks, in and out and back and forth. The flux of it fills my mind with images of somersaulting sea glass, of pebbles being dragged off the coast and regurgitated elsewhere. It fills my mind with images of other cutlery, sinking slowly out of my grasp.

I swallow hard. I worry there is sand in my throat.

"I have no ladle."

"Lies," the creature tells me, pointing a distorted finger. Something scraggled is dangling from its tip, slimy in ways I care not to linger on, and I cannot be certain if it is seaweed or flesh. "You have a ladle. Everyone does. You carry it with you. It keeps you afloat. Give it to me."

I have nothing to give. I do not have food. I do not have water. I do not even have an oar. My boat creaks beneath me, its wooden body older and twice as worn as I.

"And what," I counter, daring in ways that I do not actually feel, "are you planning to do with it, should I give it to you?"

In the nascent gloom, the sea beast's eyes are as wide and as wet as the rising moon. They glow, unimpeded by gathering clouds.

The creature tells me nothing, but I suspect.

I know.

I do not care.

"...fine."

There is no helping the water that splashes in. There is no helping how it collects.

"There is no helping you."

The puddle grows bit by bit, centimeter by centimeter, welling past the calluses on my soles and sloshing over the boils that cap my ankles.

"It is only fair, is it not? There was no helping them. You *didn't* help them. You damned them, had always intended to damn them. You saw them as sacrifices from the very start and decided their fate the same instant you stepped onboard that ship."

I hardly notice the water at first. It is not excessive, and so it is not a threat. It shouldn't be a threat. Meaningless hours gave me plenty of time to check the craft for holes; though the boat is old, it is sound. It rides the ocean's undulations with an integrity I only wish that I possessed.

"Your venture was doomed from the start, just as you always feared. Everything is as you always feared. And now this escapade is over. This is the end. There is no salvation waiting, no answers to find, no redemption to be earned. Not for one like you. Never for one like you."

I am instead possessed by other things.

"You deserve this," the creature insists, granting use of Its voice to every intrusive thought, every bitter doubt, that I have ever had. Its lilt washes over my senses, rising and falling in homage to sailors' shanties. It is elegiac and haunting. It is how islands become boulders. It is how they become powder, become nihility, I muse. It is how the sea grounds existence into oblivion.

It is...

"It is what you deserve. After all that you have done, you deserve this."

Condemnation leaches from Its every syllable, crystalline and cold when it drops. My heart drops, too, further and further down.

"After all that you have done..."

The pool beneath me ripples.

"The least you can do is die, too."

⸺⸺◦⸺⸺

"What are you?" I ask It.

Dawn is spilling in the distance, ephemeral pinks and diaphanous pales painting over the ocean's body. My own body's pinks and pales are far less lovely in comparison. This is equally true for its yellows. Its greens. I do not bother comparing our lilac tints, nor our aquamarines. Crimson effluxes into the rising shallows, wending from my veins in threads.

Idle, I admire the evanescent dance that those threads perform beneath the surface, vaguely aware of the way my wrist stings. My eyes are also stinging. Leaking.

In the country I had been leaving, there is a story about people and red threads.

Red skies in the morning, sailors take warning.

I am good at ignoring warnings, just as the creature is good at ignoring questions.

"'What am I?'" It echoes, rolling my query around as if it were driftwood thrown into the surf. I am unsurprised when the words are tossed right back at me. "What are *you?*"

There are many answers that I could give. Few are complimentary. None are worth explaining.

What skin remains around my mouth fissures into a frown, pus and blood and spittle shining in the crisscrossing crevasses that comprise its corners. Each breath is copper-flavored.

"Given that I am a dead man," I grouse, "I cannot see how that matters."

The creature sitting across from me has not yet blinked. It is a detail that I only notice now, abruptly, and for no particular reason.

I decide that this is the most upsetting thing about It.

It says, "Neither can I."

"I'm sorry," I mumble, "that this is taking so long."

My companion does not move. I have been watching It for movement, just as It has been watching me.

"Is that all you are sorry for?"

Drip, drip, drip.

Our poor boat's bottom is smelted now, the slats beneath me soggy from a coat of quicksilver. Light glints with a watery chatoyance off its surface. My shins are submerged in its luster, turning my feet into mirages. I wiggle them, but they feel no more real. There is very little about this that feels real.

That is how I know it is.

"Is this what you do?" I rasp into the afternoon, watching a particularly golden stream of sunlight make electrum of the brine. I do not think of lockets, of curls. I do not think of empty homes and emptier caskets and the journeys that these send the desperate on. I think instead of pirate treasure. I think of adventure. I think of the stories I read when I was a child, of maritime battles and swashbuckling heroes and sea monsters.

The sea monster before me folds liquescent arms, Its fingertips seeping soundlessly.

"Is this what you do?" I ask It again, the words as thin and as cracked as my lips. "You seek out the suffering and drown them in guilt?"

For the umpteenth time, we look at each other. I am still waiting for It to blink.

"You have not tried to get away," It observes in response.

If I could, I think I would laugh. I cannot. I wheeze, "Where would I go?"

"Your ladle remains whole. Solid," the beast remarks further, Its tone almost making It sound surprised. But no, It is calm. Everything here is disturbingly, distressingly calm. And so it follows that the creature should calmly admit, "I do not understand. You did nothing to it, have done nothing to it. There are no holes in it, none at all. You have not even tried to make them, despite your awareness of what is about to happen."

"Indeed, I haven't," I agree. I am uncertain what I am agreeing to. There is hardly anything worth being certain of. Nothing matters. Not now. Not since...

"Do you *want* to die?"

I do not want to say yes.

"I deserve it, like you said."

Behind me, the sun works to turn this creature into my silhouette, a grotesque parody of my lengthening shadow. I shrivel. It oozes, reflecting on all that I am and all that I am not before It begrudgingly hums, "Yours is a strong moral compass."

I still cannot laugh. I do manage a snort.

"Suppose so. Not as helpful as a literal one would be."

"Why haven't you made excuses?" It wonders aloud, less a question and more a critique. Its face lacks the capacity to scowl, but I choose to pretend It is doing so. "There are so many you could have made, a plethora you could have chosen from. Poor visibility. Outdated equipment. Misheard orders. Any of these.

All of these. People would have believed you. *You* would have believed you, given time to drill the lie. That is how the human conscious works."

Beyond the lip of our lifeboat, the skyline stretches into eternity. A promise of *forever* resonates behind my ears.

"Maybe," I contend. "But that wouldn't have made it the truth."

⸺◦○◦⸺

The thought occurs later. The question after that.

"Do you still think I deserve this?"

Seawater sluices from the creature's torso, drains out of Its wrists and down Its nape.

It is answer enough.

⸺◦○◦⸺

"Are you... *them*?"

In the night, Its eyes are twin moons again, reflections of a reflection that can somehow direct the endless tides. Push-pull, push-pull, and my sodden skin starts to slough from the undersides of my thighs.

It confesses, "No."

"...oh."

The truth surprises me more than I thought it would; I did not realize how deeply my assumptions had rooted until I felt something crack inside my bones. Like raw pearls in shells, the emotions that were hiding in my marrow have been brusquely and wholly exposed, acid heaving up my gullet in a surge I cannot stop. It empties me. I *feel* empty, for none of this has mattered.

Nothing matters.

I collapse against the side of the boat, saline eating at my hips. Something else has eaten at the stars, and I am surrounded by a midnight most tenebrous. It cocoons me, enshrouds me. It binds me like a winding sheet, woven from both the tangible and the incorporeal.

When it squeezes, I choke out, "Do you... Do you mind if I pretend you are?"

Truly, nothing matters.

"If it eases your conscience."

"Will you tell me... what you really are...?"

"You know what I really am."

"...are you me?"

"'This is the part where you try to escape,' you said. 'I think you are the reason I am here,' I replied."

"And do you still think that now?"

"Being honest," I slur, "I don't know... if what I am doing now... truly qualifies as 'thinking' anymore."

My head floats upon the ocean's crest, bobbing in lieu of the boat. The boat is gone. It is all gone. It had gurgled, gentle as a baby, before disappearing like so much else from my life. Only the creature remains.

"You are... the reason I am here," I burble, and my saying so is not quite a contradiction. It is not quite the truth, either; it is as figurative as it is literal. It is...

It *is*...

"Lies," It reproves a second time, the ebb-flow accusation no louder than the kiss of the sea on the shore. Memories and hallucinations amalgamate. The beast looms above me, Its face scant inches from my own, and only in this moment do I realize how It is crying. How it has always been crying. "*You* are the reason *I* am here."

There is electrum in Its eyes.

It closes them when I close mine.

Major Key Inspirations:
Legends of Umibozu

xii. fæge

1. "What are you doing?"

Marwick expected this question. Has been waiting for it, in his way—wondering when the villagers' curiosity would get the better of them, would force *someone* to engage with him. He had anticipated accusations, shouting. Maybe even someone chasing him from the cemetery with a crucifix in their hands, or while brandishing a shovel above their head.

But now that he is being asked—*actually* asked, *finally* asked—he cannot think of how to answer.

It takes him a minute of floundering to settle on the truth.

"I, um,. I'm cleaning the graves," Marwick says, voice low with nerves and weak from disuse. A flurry of lichen flakes free from the brush that he clutches, loosened from worn bristles by his trembles. "The... the ocean air, the salt, and the moisture. It makes the headstones old before their time."

The young man who stands before him—sun-kissed and sinewy, with eyes too dark to fathom—cocks his head as Marwick rambles, sending a wave of damp curls cascading over his shoulder. In their silky pitch they match the nearby sea, and Marwick thinks them a striking complement to that brooding,

Stygian horizon. Certainly they are a prettier color than the dirty spume of his own hair.

Before wistful admiration can sharpen into envy, the stranger asks, "Why?"

"'Why?'" Marwick falters, bemused. "I... I just said—"

"No. That's not what I'm asking. Why are *you* cleaning them?" the other man clarifies, the shallow furrow between his brows becoming cavernous. "Do you work for the church?"

"Oh! N-no."

"Do these graves belong to your family?"

"I don't—um. Well. No." Half-hidden behind and half-blended into the restored white of a tombstone, Marwick dares to meet this outsider's gaze, taking note of the feelings that churn within it. The confusion is telling, and the absence of disgust is a nice surprise, but it is the utter lack of recognition that makes it clear that he is not native to this place.

Marwick suspected as much. Although he does not really *know* anyone in the village, they are all people familiar to him. This man, in his elegant breeches and blouse and cape, with his swallet eyes and untamed hair, is not.

"So, then," the unfamiliar man frowns. "Why?"

Marwick glances briefly at his hand. It is still shaking, just a little. But wrapped around a brush like this, it could almost pass as human.

"Because," he says, "I didn't want them to be lonely."

⸺◆⸺

2. *"An' it sall come to pass on a simmer's day,*

When the sin shines het on evera stane,
That I will tak my little young son,
An' teach him for to swim the faem..."

"You have a lovely voice."

Marwick startles at the greeting, the note he had been holding so delicately between his teeth cracking in alarm. Metronomic scraping stutters when the tool tumbles from his grip.

"Oh," he squeaks, cringing behind today's limestone marker. The ancient grave is tangled in the thick of the root-threaded hill, tucked away behind a hawthorn tree, and he had not thought his singing loud enough to undermine its use as a hideaway. In his ears, the rushing surf is overwhelmed by rushing blood. "You're back."

The black-eyed man peers from around the other side of the tree.

"I am," he confirms, blithely readjusting the skin he wears draped around his shoulders. Its sleekness catches what light filters through the clouds, and Marwick is reminded of the way that sunshine pools, nacreous and oily atop the water.

Swallowing, Marwick tucks his hands between his knees. "Um. Why?"

"I have family here."

"Oh." That makes sense, Marwick supposes. Though, even when he squints, he cannot find any hereditary connection between the stranger's features and those of whom he has lived amongst since birth. Tentatively, Marwick presses, "Do they... live in the village, or...?"

"You made their acquaintance during our previous meeting."

"Oh," Marwick says again, cringing. That makes *more* sense, all things considered. "I'm sorry, I—sorry for your loss, and... and for touching those graves without permission. I didn't mean any disrespect. It had just been... It had been so long since I saw anyone there, and the headstones were looking so—that is, I didn't—"

"You didn't want them to be lonely," the young man finishes. His voice is light when he speaks. Always light, always gentle, the words drifting atop currents of air. He has not moved from his spot behind the tree. Has not even blinked, as far as Marwick can tell, and his hair is yet too heavy with moisture to be rustled by the breeze.

Marwick's own uncanny curls, buoyant as foam, float about his temples. Distant though they are, the waves that crash against the shoreline's crags nearly drown him out. "I'm sorry."

"Why are you *sorry*?"

"I... just am, I suppose."

"You needn't be," the other shrugs. Marwick watches his strong shoulders lift, lower. Lower still. With great deliberation, the ethereal stranger descends, stopping only when he is eye level with the crouching Marwick. Submerged beneath its shade, the hawthorn casts diaphanous patterns across their faces, their silhouettes trimmed by filtered, lacy light. "It was a fair call. Yesterday was my first visit to the site. And I can't imagine anyone having come before me."

Branches undulate. Leaves froth. Marwick is not sure how to react to any of this, and so settles for a third, "Oh."

"Do you have a name?" the stranger queries, crossing his legs in the grass.

"I do."

"...may I know what it is?" he prompts, inhumanly patient, after a moment of silence becomes a full minute.

Marwick blushes up to his ears, barely biting back a fourth, humiliated, *oh*. But he would rather be assumed an idiot than admit that no one has ever needed his name before. That no one has ever bothered to ask.

"Marwick," he mumbles. "Marwick Thomson."

The other man nods.

"'Marwick,'" he echoes, almost contemplatively. "Marwick, caretaker of lonely graves."

Marwick considers protesting the epithet. Ultimately, he cannot but acknowledge that he has been called worse. "What about you?"

"Me?"

"What is your name?"

"Ah."

There is something reassuring in seeing his surprise reflected upon another's face. Not in a cruel sense; Marwick takes no pleasure in his struggles. But it is heartening to think that maybe Marwick isn't the only one. Maybe this man has never been asked his name, either. Maybe this is something that they share.

A bond, even one forged from sadness, is still a bond.

As Marwick considers this—considers other ways that they might be similar—the beautiful stranger smiles, revealing pearl-colored canines.

"Kale," he says, like he is making a decision. "I am called Kale."

"Kale...?"

"Kale," Marwick is told again, with a placid, purposeful firmness, and so he leaves it at that.

—◆—

3. The cemetery sprawls as only dead things can: shamelessly, serene. In its own way, the expansive plot reminds Marwick of the ocean, and sometimes he cannot help but consider its roils and swells of blue-green grass an extension of the adjacent sea.

A fog rolls in, misty, tidal crests that coil between engraved stone stacks. Fucoid growths threaten to capsize old graves. Gulls make their noisy rounds, and no one thinks of the wooden vessels that molder below.

No one except Marwick. If Marwick allows his mind to drift, he feigns he can feel more than the autumnal cold between his joints. There is also that abyss. That *gravity* that exists beneath the veneer of this world, pulling everything down and apart and *together* towards some secret, shared fate.

It does not hide. It does not threaten. Its presence helps maintain the framework of existence, and it hurts and it comforts in equal measure.

Marwick does not know if there is a word to describe how this sensation makes him feel, but he is tempted to use *nostalgic.*

"I won't, though. That sounds silly," he acknowledges, sheepish, as he makes a show of digging through his bag. There is hardly anything in the tattered satchel; his fingers are already folded around his cleaning supplies. But Kale had again appeared from the ether and is watching too closely for Marwick to risk revealing his hands.

Kale fixes the lay of the cape swathed around him, tautening the pelt until it moves like a second skin against his arms.

"It isn't," he murmurs. The clouds are thickening, threatening a true rain, and when Kale tucks his head beneath the mouth of his hood, he runs the risk of vanishing back into the gray. "It isn't silly."

"For something to be nostalgic, it must first be experienced. I can't even *name* this."

"Names aren't important."

"Yes, you'd think that, 'just Kale.'"

"Well, they aren't. Not in the face of experience."

"Yes, *precisely*. You can't be nostalgic for something you've never experienced," Marwick argues, good-humored in his exasperation. "And to the best of my knowledge, I haven't *died* before."

"Haven't you?" Kale counters, settling atop an unsanctified stone. "What are you made of? What am I made of? Unfinished loam and seafoam, that's what. Ashes and dust and flotsam, ground up by the flow of time and tides. We live on and eat from the wreckages that others have left behind, taking their ruins into our own, and in so doing become a singular being—an ouroboros comprised of memories and parts that are ever in flux. A loop of connections and condemnations entwined inside a lone skin, birthed and rebirthed. Dismantled and rearranged. Again and again."

Although he can navigate its yard with a captain's confidence, Marwick himself is not of the church. Rather than horrified, he is tickled by Kale's pragmatic blasphemy.

"This is an oddly deep conversation," he comments, "to be having with someone I met but three days ago."

Kale grins, his eyes like sinkholes beneath the shadow of his cowl. "I am certain we could yet plunge deeper."

---

4. Even so, there is something to be said for shallower conversations.

Kale begins their fourth day with a remark on the weather. Soon after, they segue into a discussion about seasonal fish, and a debate over local fishermen. Eventually, that dissolves into gossip about village residents, their jobs and their families.

Then, as is his way, Kale pulls Marwick in over his head with one question.

"Who runs the lighthouse?" he asks, gesturing to the pale obelisk that looms in the middle distance. A different sort of monument, ostensibly dedicated to life rather than death.

Marwick responds by scrubbing harder at the day's headstone. The extra vigor is unnecessary. It is also telling.

"It's yours?"

"Who runs it and who it belongs to are two different questions with two different answers."

"So it *is* yours."

"I suppose. Technically. Yes," Marwick sighs. "It was my mother's. Or her family's, anyway. Her father inherited it from his father when he passed, and she inherited it from her father when *he* passed, and I inherited it from her when... well. But I... No one really *runs* it. Not anymore."

Leaning against the opposite side of a half-scoured marker, Kale waits. Silent. Listening.

"The Northern Lighthouse Board saw to it that the light was changed a few years before I was born, around when the century turned," Marwick mumbles. Swiftly after, he adds, "And I'm not ungrateful! I'm not. It would have been impossible for me to take care of everything 'the traditional way.' Especially on my own. I never knew my father, you see, nor his family. I've no siblings, and the people in the village... they keep their distance. So. The important thing is that the new light allowed my mother more time to take care of me, and then later, more time for me to take care of my mother. But she's gone now, and the electricity isn't. There's... well, not *nothing* to do, but *less*. I'm paid more to keep to myself than to keep the light."

A *thump* punctuates this claim, Kale's crown falling back against the headstone.

"Why?" he asks.

What a question that is.

"What about you?" Marwick counters, maybe a little too loudly. The white caps of his knuckles waver around his brush. "You said your family is from here?"

"I said that I have family buried here," Kale corrects, still in those mild tones. A finger traces the uneven edges of the animal skin that warms him. "I am from further north. Closer to Orkney."

"So then why—?"

"My mother... remarried," he explains. The word is delicately chosen, handled with the sort of care indicative of very fragile lies. Marwick purses his lips, sympathy trickling like ice down his spine. "My father, siblings, and I weren't able to do anything about it. Father tried, but... It wasn't safe. She passed a few years ago."

"I'm sorry," Marwick offers. It is not enough, of course. It never is. But it is all that he has to give.

Kale does not accept. He is not unkind about it; his smile is an enigmatic mixture of concern and charm when he glances at Marwick from over his shoulder. Those pelagic eyes may hide volumes, but nothing within their crush is cruel.

"Why do you do that?" he asks. A breeze blusters through, current-strong. It sets Kale's hair dancing, dried strands swaying like kelp. "Why do you keep apologizing for things over which you had no control?"

"I—that's not it." Flushing, Marwick ducks further behind the grave. "It's... I'm *empathizing*. It's sad that you were separated from your mother. That you are only able to visit her again now that she's gone."

"My mother is not why I'm here."

A pause. Marwick decides that there is more laughter than incredulity in Kale's retort, which makes it easier to keep from scowling at his amused companion. Having twisted bodily around, Kale is now propped up on his knees, chin cushioned by the arms that he has crossed atop the headstone.

"We've not yet swum together, but I'm already afraid for you," he teases. "I hope that you dive with more accuracy than you jump to conclusions."

His gaze upon Marwick is ceaseless, unblinking, glittering. Radiant as moonlight over mercurial waters. And yet, for reasons that Marwick cannot fully articulate, he finds himself thinking more of sea twinkle than the holy phosphorescence of a living human soul.

This is still preferable to acknowledging how his own features burn.

"Well, all right, fine," Marwick pouts, slipping his fists inside his sleeves. "If you're such a master at navigating conversations, Kale, I nominate you to captain this one for a while."

Kale smirks like a cresting wave.

"It's true that I chose this place because of my mother," he explains, "but she is not the reason that I am here. That would have been a short trip indeed."

"The dead don't have much to say to visitors," Marwick concedes, trying not to look too pleased with himself when Kale chuckles. He tries further not to linger on how pretty Kale is, curled and comfortable atop the sun-warmed stone. "But if that's the case, then what brought you here?"

There is a brackishness to Kale's sigh that Marwick cannot help but notice. Suddenly somber, Kale sinks back below the camber of the grave.

"I have seven days," he tells Marwick, "to mate."

Marwick is grateful to the marrow of his bones that Kale is already turned around. Not even the lighthouse's incandescent bulbs glow as brightly as his face does now.

"Oh. Um. S-so you're... you're a sailor... on shore leave?"

"Something like that," Kale drawls, sounding as discomforted by his predicament as Marwick. "It's... I'm not sure what to call it. A family tradition? A genetic obligation? I don't know. I don't like it. I don't... I didn't want to come at all. But having had only so much choice in the matter, I tried my best to mitigate the situation."

This time, it is Marwick who peeks over the headstone, allowing the barest tips of his fingers to curl around its wind-worn curves.

"What do you mean?" he presses, encouraging. The slumping Kale glowers at the salt-tinged skyline.

"I was taught," he mutters, "that on land I would have 'great seductive powers.' Powers that would make this whole charade... easier. I was told that those who are 'dissatisfied with their lives' would flock to me, compelled to... want to have my children. I figured if I spent the week hiding somewhere without many people, I could avoid the worst of it. Then I could go home, and I wouldn't need to worry about it again for seven years."

Marwick recognizes that he needs to respond. How, though? He rolls portions of a confession over in his head, examining individual words from multiple angles and marveling at the truth that has started to take shape in his mind.

Eventually, assiduously, Marwick eases himself around the grave. Sits, demure, beside the bowed and flustered Kale, a hand splayed between them in the coarse teal grass.

And Kale notices. Marwick sees the instant that Kale notices. Feels those velveteen eyes drag up his body, over his face.

"I'm sorry," Marwick says for the umpteenth time, with a calmness belied by quivering fingers. "You are very handsome, but I don't want to have children. With anybody."

The bark of laughter that escapes Kale startles him more than it does Marwick. Mortified, Kale stoppers the sound with a palm. His cheeks are the crimson of a maritime sunset.

"You apologize for the queerest things," Kale chokes, trying for chiding. Failing. If anything, he sounds delighted.

Marwick shrugs.

"I just wouldn't want you thinking there's anything wrong with your 'great seductive powers,'" he wryly comforts. Kale snorts again, his attention drifting back to Marwick's malformed hand. How its webbing quavers, how the scaly skin shines. How closely it is braced to Kale's thigh.

Peeling his own hand from his face, Kale hesitates, his breathing slow.

"You called me *handsome*," he realizes. Belated, but with something effervescent fizzing beneath his shock.

In turn, Marwick feels a tiny bubble of emotion—embarrassment? Elation?—rise in his chest. He clears his throat. "I guess I did."

"You think I'm handsome?"

"I do have eyes."

Kale thrills at this, fiddling bashfully with the hem of his pelt. "Are you... dissatisfied with your life, Marwick?"

There is a beat. Of anxious hearts. Of far-off waves. Marwick focuses as best he can on the outline of the lighthouse: a single, cloud-white column that he can sometimes believe keeps the heavens themselves from falling. *A different sort of monument*, his family's livelihood and resting place, which has saved more souls than it has snuffed, and yet—

And yet.

"No, I'm not," Marwick says. "Not right now."

Something inside his chest gutters. Fingers are brushing against the back of his wrist, cool and smooth and inescapable, eager as an undertow. They threaten to drag him under, down and apart and *together, and yet*—

They feel like a lifeline.

⸺⧫⸺

5. It is the end of the Sabbath, and the sky is the rich, clear blue of consecrated stained glass. They are on the beach, the church and its yard having been reserved for more pious folk, but it hardly feels like a change.

"What is the ocean, really," Marwick supposes, "if not the vastest of graves?"

Kale looks as if he has some answer to this, but keeps it to himself; nothing he might try to add would change that basic truth.

The tower of the lighthouse stretches silvery over the sea.

"Go into the light," Kale whispers, a guiding beam glimmering off the surface of his pupils. It illumes nothing of the impossible profundity that his eyes contain. "That's what the devout say, isn't it? To those who are dying. I suppose that means my family never belonged to any god, for we were always told the opposite. *If you want to be saved, turn your back to the light.*"

"And yet, here you are."

"Here I am."

"Were... Were you looking to die?"

"Hmm. I wonder," Kale muses, in the same airy way that he says everything. "Certainly I had a better idea of what I *didn't* want to find than what I did. But perhaps, maybe, I *was* looking for the end of a story. One that my father used to tell."

"About the lighthouse," Marwick says. It isn't a question. And yet, Kale answers all the same.

"Yes. According to my father, fire used to burn up there. *Real* fire, hot and alive. And so the light that it created was hot and alive too, flickering as it did on this littoral candle's wick-tip. This held true for eons.

"But then, one night, the light changed. It turned steady. Soulless. Became the color of bleached-bone, sharper than the rocks from which it was meant to protect sailors.

"That's when Father took to calling it *The Gravestone*. Or so he claimed. Whenever I asked why, he said it was because this artificial light 'marked the end of natural beauty.' We would pass its shadow, and he'd lament how mankind would regret succumbing to this technological plague. 'The people on land will blind themselves on manufactured rays,' he'd say, 'and begin to long in vain for the oblivion that they've lost.'

"Well. I can't speak to that loss, of course. Nor can I speak to that longing. I was so young, then. In my memories, the lighthouse has only ever painted the night in colors of death. Still, I don't think that's why Father granted the light that name. Rather, I... I was told by one of my sisters that during our travels, our mother saw the new light from afar and was enchanted and disgusted and confused in equal measure. It pulled at her like an abyss. Like gravity. There was nothing for it, she decided, but to investigate.

"She never came home again."

Water beats against the shore. Marwick is not sure what to say. Briefly he considers *I'm sorry*, but in the end decides against it.

This is not about him.

Instead, he grazes Kale's hand with his own, a subtle, breaching motion. It imitates the possessiveness of the waves. Swells shift the shingles of the shore's red shale, but nothing stretches far enough, rises high enough, to touch Kale. Not like Marwick has.

Kale grins. The satin fur of his hide glints in the gloaming, its dappled pales liquescent where the pelt drips off his shoulders.

"Can you swim?" he asks, a conspiratorial edge to his playfulness. Marwick makes a show of shrugging.

"Oh, I'm still trying to figure out how to get into the water."

"What?"

"Well, as you know, I can't jump, I can't dive..."

"*Cheeky*," Kale admonishes, although the rebuke is somewhat undermined by their harmonized giggles. "I'm being serious! Do you swim?"

"No. Not recently. Not in years," Marwick admits. "When I was a child, I swam every day. But it made me feel... It filled me with... I'm not sure how to describe it."

"'Nostalgia?'" Kale guesses.

"Yes."

They listen to the ocean breathe. They watch the lighthouse's steady pulse. The full body of night envelops them beneath its gossamer skin, and within that embrace the earth and sky and land and water are enfolded into one great ouroboros.

Kale and Marwick are not yet earth. They are not yet sky or land or water, either. So when Kale's smallest finger hooks around Marwick's, Marwick feels it in his heart: a sharp, painful reminder of their present severance. Of the spaces between. Of the loneliness that had, in truth, only ever been his own.

Like everything that is not-yet-dead, they are so far apart—and he realizes that he hates it, even as that touch anchors them together.

"Do you dance?" Kale wonders.

"My mother did," Marwick tells him. In his mind's eye, he can see the ghost of her; his smile is slight and haunted. "That's how she met my father, apparently. He saw her dancing on the beach, and Ma said he just joined in. The way she told it, he was lovely. And kind. And free-spirited. That last thing in particular. After a week of courtship, he was gone."

"And he *didn't* come back?" Kale gasps. This detail seems to bother him more than it does Marwick. "He never came back for you?"

"Should he have?"

"*Yes.*"

Not even Marwick's mother had expressed this sentiment with such conviction. He forces the instinctive apology back down his throat.

"Do you sing?" Marwick asks instead. The boldness of the redirection surprises him as much as it does Kale. "You've heard me sing. So... Do you?"

Four more fingers slip through Marwick's, agonizingly gentle when they skim over the tissues that web his hand. A tug, and Marwick follows, moored to Kale's swaying hips.

"Only when I'm dancing."

⸺◦⸺

6. A squall hits on the penultimate day of Kale's visit.

It is sudden, as such things often are. Neither the kirkyard nor the beach offers much in the way of shelter, and while Marwick generally considers the lighthouse no better than the eye of a storm, that is because it is usually empty.

It isn't empty now.

Kale is here. Kale fills the parlor with laughter, with warmth. Kale has a fire roaring by the time that Marwick finishes making tea, and announces as much by calling to the kitchen:

"Will you tell me my fortune, Marwick?"

Rain sluices down dirty windows, reducing the rest of the world to gramophone static. It makes everything that happens in this room louder. Realer, somehow. Marwick stumbles in the doorway to the parlor, nearly dropping the mugs that he carries.

"Of we two, Kale," he huffs, regaining his composure, "I rather think that you are better suited to do that. I'm—I wasn't raised like... I'm only half..."

"Nonsense," Kale sniffs, prim in the nest of blankets he has arranged before the hearth. Flamelight shimmers golden over his face, his arms, its natural smolder a stark contrast to the mechanical blaze of the lighthouse. There is a metaphor in that, but Marwick ignores it in favor of settling on the floor next to Kale and passing him his drink. "You swim and dance. You sing better than I do. I'm confident that you could predict my future, if you tried."

Tea swirls in the basin of Marwick's chipped cup, red as fate. Red as blood. He considers its depths, and its dregs, and what it dredges out of him.

"Sometimes," he confesses, "when Ma made tea, I'd watch the ripples. The way those bands expanded, out and out, until they swallowed each other. Until they consumed themselves. Until everything became one again. And if I… if I watched long enough…"

"Yes?"

Marwick's brow pinches beneath unruly bangs. He sets his mug aside. "Kale, I—What if… What if I don't…?"

"If you don't want to try, that's all right," Kale assures, placing his own tea next to Marwick's. But Marwick shakes his head.

"That's not it," he insists. Were he not so worried, he might have sounded shy. "What if I don't see myself there? What if I'm not part of your future?"

"Then I suppose you'll have been right about your prophetic abilities."

Something in the fire *pops*. It is hushed by the storm. Their tea settles to flatness, twin surfaces reflecting the same darkness.

"You already know, don't you.""Hmm?"

"I've heard that… more powerful folk. They know their futures. How they will die. Is that true?" Marwick murmurs, not without pity. "Do you already know how you'll die?"

Despite the chill, Kale has divested himself of his cloak, tucking its brindled browns and blacks around Marwick. It is a display of tenderness that warms him more than any fire ever could. Because this—*this*—is something that *Marwick* knows. He knows what Kale's gesture means.

He *knows*.

Idly, Marwick flexes his fingers along the fur's grain, delighting in the mottled pinks that appear high on Kale's cheeks. The skin is unbearably soft. It is gorgeous. Kale is gorgeous. And Marwick might believe that he is gorgeous, too, when Kale looks at him like this, with eyes made crepuscular by embers and emotion.

"Yes," Kale rasps.

"Yes?" Marwick caresses the cowl as he might a lover's face, and Kale whimpers before managing to speak again.

"Yes," he says a second time. Hoarsely, melodiously, he admits, "Yes, I do. Just as I know how *you* will die. Just as I know how *everyone* I meet will die."

"Oh." Marwick mulls on this revelation for a moment, gaze tracing the shape of his bestial hands where they rest atop Kale's pelt. There is brine lingering in the corners of his mouth. He can taste it when he asks, "Will mine—will I—be lonely?"

"*No.*"

Inexorable as the tide, Kale rushes forward, gentle, warm. Overwhelming. Salt-sweet lips brush across Marwick's, and Marwick cannot breathe.

Marwick never wants to breathe again.

"Marwick Thomson," Kale promises, as together they drown beneath roughly heaped blankets, "by the seven seas, I swear. You will never be lonely again."

Somewhere beyond the tempestuous horizon, the sun sets on Kale's sixth day.

———◦———

7. The shallows swirl about their shins, blooming around their ankles like funerary flowers.

Crimson, crystalline, gilt-white and ichorous: iridescent petals lap up their legs, over their knees, and Marwick has never felt more grounded than he does in this moment, as an undercurrent lifts his feet off the sand, helping Kale guide him further from the shore.

"Unfinished loam and seafoam," Marwick remembers—thoughtful, dreamy—floating in that liminal space between sky and earth, pulled along by the flow of time and tides. "A singular being, comprised of memories and parts that are ever in flux."

Kale's hand tightens around his own.

"A singular being," he agrees, his voice echoing as waves do against gravel coasts. "A loop of connections and condemnations entwined inside a lone skin."

"Better *a lone*," Marwick reasons, "than *alone*."

"Yes," Kale beams. Dawn sparkles off a mouthful of pointed teeth. The water has reached their waists. It ripples, red as fate, red as blood. "Are you ready?"

"I think so," Marwick says, drawn to an oscillating still beside Kale. Before Kale. Chest to chest and heart to heart, so close that even the ocean cannot find space between them. "It has been a while, though. Since I last did any swimming."

"As long as you're better at it than jumping."

"I'm taking you down with me," Marwick intones, dry enough to be ironic. Kale's answering laugh is as stunning as the cold, as the surf and the breeze and the hide that he arranges so meticulously around their bodies: an inverse mortal vale.

Marwick can think of no more beautiful way to die.

"Come," Kale whispers into his ear, pulling the sealskin shroud over their heads. "I'll teach you how to swim the foam."

And as one, they sink into the abyss.

Major Key Inspiration:
"The Great Silkie of Sule Skerry"

xiii. catacombs

It is my sister's good luck that she dies first.

No one expected me to outlive her. I hadn't expected to, either. I'm strong, I suppose, from a childhood of chopping and hewing wood, but despite the best efforts of my teachers, I've never been skilled at close-quarters combat.

My fingers are for delicate work. That's what Father always said. Then he'd grin and tell my sister that, when the time came, she should be sure to aim for my carotid, rather than my radial arteries. I'd laugh and she'd promise she would.

Had the decision been made in a more *traditional* fashion, I believe she would have kept that promise. I would have been the one to die. It was a certainty in my mind, one in which I had taken a great deal of comfort.

But then illness came. When it left, my sister was its escort.

And so, here I stand. Hale and healthy in my best robes and new beads, protective charms wound around my arms and herbs threaded through my hair. Earlier, and with great pageantry, the High Priestess strapped a knife to my side: a ceremonial blade of silver and ostentation, with archaic symbols carved into its handle.

I know from having held the knife that it isn't all that heavy. Not really. But in this moment, it weighs upon me more than my sister's death did. More than my sister's corpse *does*.

After the knife, her body was tied to my back with red cord, the rope's girth tangling over my belly in a mess of respooled intestines. More effort was put into the knots that cover my sister, the High Priestess's brother lacing a veritable web over her shoulders, around her ribs, and down her spin. The design's ostentation serves as a substitute for lacerations I did not inflict. For blood I did not spill.

Her arms are draped around me in a parodied embrace. I watch a droplet of perfume roll down her index finger, peeling from its tip like liquified flesh.

There is a gravity to this. To all of this. To this corpse, to this ritual. To the Catacombs themselves. I feel drawn into this opening in the earth, pulled towards the collapsar core of this cavern. Even the sunrise's purest rays can do no more than ripple the surface of that looming, celestial gloom.

Black and white, life and death. Lessons on dualism my sister will never get to learn. Existence's dichotomies occupy my thoughts as neighbors begin to file into rows behind me, backs to the light and eyes on the darkness. The sun's warmth is steadily melting their shadows into tar, and I try to distract myself by watching the slow, sticky strings of their extremities ooze across the desert clay.

When dawn becomes full morning, this congealing facsimile of community reaches my sandals. They stain my feet.

These are my friends. My family. People who have already made their pilgrimages into the Catacombs stand side-by-side with those who are eagerly awaiting their turn in the void. It is bizarre to think that, not so very long ago, I was one of those dreaming youths myself, wondering about the part my cadaver would play on *That Day*.

On *this* day.

The sands have shifted. Time has shifted. And the infinite possibilities that once comprised my future have shifted to align with obligations and inevitabilities, creating a singular path that wends towards my destiny.

At the start of that path, the High Priestess stands, smiling. The expression is wide enough to crinkle the bandages that cover her empty sockets.

"Are you prepared?" she asks.

Whether or not she will believe me, I know better than to tell her the truth. "Yes."

I try not to stare at the coal smudge that has marred the outline of her right eye, leaving the muslin gray. It helps when she steps to the side, choosing to walk next to me as I approach the mouth of the cave.

Bells sing around the High Priestess' weathered ankles. Bangles chitter on translucent wrists. They are as much a warning as the few words she offers.

"Choose wisely."

Some wistful incarnation of fondness has caught in the corners of her lips, much how a dreamcatcher snares nightmares. It festers when the High Priestess lingers, standing on the edge of what she cannot see. What she could not see, not ever again, even *if* her brother had not robbed her of her sight.

I am uninjured. My sister could pass for sleeping.

The High Priestess' brother is standing to my left, his white teeth dyed scarlet by daybreak. Excess luminance dribbles off his canines, down his chin, until it reaches the antiquated shaft of the spear that remains impaled through his throat.

When he echoes the High Priestess's sentiment, air and vowels leak through his lesions, unraveling his words so that each is heard three times.

"Choose wisely. Choose wisely. *Choose wisely.*"

Although the eyes that look into mine are comprised of the same muscles and fluids, his gaze is more abhuman than his sister's sketched stare could ever be, and I fear whatever-it-is he sees in me, just as I fear whatever-it-is I see in him: that sentience which lurks in the depths of dilated pupils, transplendent and transcendental.

Like a glass shard, the High Priestess's brother reflects radiance without creating it, mirrors humanity without being it, and his voice is suffused with wheezy omniscience when he adds:

"It is not only your own fate that you will be deciding… not only your own fate that you will be deciding… *your own fate that you will be deciding.*"

⸺◆⸺

Inside the Catacombs, torchlight flickers and flits, a fickle touch on antediluvian stone. Here, gone. Gold to obsidian.

In those brief moments, I notice swirling minerals, crystalline strata. Handprints and footprints and fingerprints that have smeared like the High Priestess's lashes, smoky shapes that suggest so much and tell so little. Jagged edges point out details, while moss spores and glowworms create constellations over runes, cuneiform, hieroglyphs. There are stories here—layer upon sedimentary layer of history, remnants of ritual written on the rocks—and a Gordian knot of timelines with loose ends that I have been charged to follow.

I obey, sensing as I do every gaze that follows after.

The first I find are indistinguishable from those natural mounds and boulders that are piled along the walls.

They are smooth, featureless. Lumpy and crumbling. Only the glossy patina of skin-oil that remains upon their contours hints at what they had once been.

In the dim, these stones resemble graves. I am grateful that the air does not taste of decay, even as I wish it did. The torch that I clutch in my fist begins to quaver, its flames like hair in deep water. It is a struggle to breathe.

But that would not excuse a failure to introduce myself.

"Hear me, all who share this profane tomb!" I call into oblivion. *"I stand before you, the champion of battle! See how I am laden with glory, with purpose, with the corpse of my fallen adversary! See how she resembles you in stillness! Already, she too is nameless and forgotten! What has history taught you? What have you learned from abandonment? That only the victors' will shall see you evoked once more! My will, and mine alone! This is the conqueror's privilege: to decide who is honored, who is remembered, who is damned to rot into obscurity. So I ask you, you*

gathered and forsaken divine, to submit to me. Worship me, that I might worship you!"

This final shout lingers, haunting the space between my nose and my torch. It spirals, misty; it fades, evanescent. But though its ghost vanishes, the message's spirit lives on. Through the labyrinthine black, I can hear my invitation resound and reverberate, becoming a cacophony comprised of one voice, one prayer, one answer:

Worship me. Worship me. Worship me. Worship me.

When next I stop, it is before an orgy of masonry bodies. They reach for me from a northern niche, their petrified arms turned partly to ash. It is to the one with three and a half fingers that I ask, "What is your offering? What will you give?"

There is a pause before It answers. But when It speaks, It does so in a voice that is mine, and isn't mine, and is and isn't the voice of everyone I've ever known: a distant, too-close whisper in the back of my mind.

I will give you health. Your body will know vigor and your mind will know strength. With me, no sickness shall touch you for all of your years.

The stench of preservatives still clings to my sister's corpse, rancidly sweet. I glower at Its mockery before turning away.

"Two down and four to the back. What will you offer?"

I will give you sunshine. I will give you verdant greens. Flowers and ferns and food from the earth, all the magic that the soil possesses. All the beauty and the power.

Its cooing resonates in the chamber of my skull as much as in the pit of Its entrapment. There are serpentine shadows slithering in that nook, twisting around underdefined stoles. As I watch, a desperate thread of nothingness detaches, stretches, and is rewound into the abyss.

I step back, my torch hissing.

There are plenty more niches. There are hollows and crannies and alcoves, too. There are natural shelves and manmade shelves and no shelves at all, but instead rows upon rows of splintered remains.

I think of teeth. Of gullets and bellies and insides turned out.

Then I walk on.

The pattern continues. I can't say for how long. Time is meaningless in this place.

"What will you offer?"

I will give you command over your fellows. The valor to lead, the wisdom to guide, the courage to inspire. To the humans you will be like a king, and to the kings you will be like a god.

"What will you offer?"

I will give you love. Passion and pleasure, kindness and concern. Never again will you know a cold bed, a lonely night, a friendless day. Choose me, and you shall bask in devotion until your dying breath.

"What will you offer?"

I will give you gold. Coins, jewels, silks, marble, ivory. All the precious treasures your purse can hold, never depleting, never in want. Your cup shall runneth over until you are drowning in luxuries.

"What will you offer?"

I will give you luck. Better than skill, and more reliable than mercy. Fortune's favor shall be yours in every endeavor, however poor your odds or foolish your gamble.

I keep walking.

⚫

The effigy at the crossroads is no more or less decrepit than any of the others I have passed.

When scrutinizing It, I find myself thinking that—possibly—It is Mesopotamian. Or—more possibly—It is Babylonian. Or—most possible of all—It is so incomprehensibly old that there is no longer any record of the people who once revered It, nor of the circumstances that saw It exiled to the Catacombs. War, plague, genocide; it's all pitiful, it's all boggling. It's all impossible to wrap my mind around: how the ground on which my society was built is comprised of tiered apocalypses.

Millenniums have stripped away most of Its definition, but the idol before me has managed to retain some of Its limbs, a chunk of Its hair. A few small details still remain on Its face, like the suggestion of a nose. Looking lower, I notice toes. The scoring on Its torso likely denotes missing jewelry, and though Its wedge-shaped body does not quite reach my knees, It radiates an aura that both enervates and imposes.

I stand before the carved deity, deliberating, silent. Shadows dance around us with devilish dexterity, their gossamer tendrils prehensile in the gloom. After countless hours, after so much dissatisfaction, there is little expectation in the demand when I intone, "What will you offer?"

For a beat, my mind echoes with emptiness.

Then:

I will give you nothing.

•◦•

If there are issues to be had with my sister's corpse—lingering bacteria, or stiffness, or muscular deterioration—, the entity makes no complaints about them.

On the contrary, It seems greatly pleased. I'm not sure It even noticed the line that my ceremonial knife gouged into Its new Vessel's palm.

Ripping a scrap of cloth from my now-defiled robes, I wonder if I ought to offer It a bandage. Or maybe I should wrap Its palm after finishing with my own? If I don't, will the cut heal? If I do, will it scar? Will my sister's body suddenly remember how to bleed?

The blood that stains our matching gashes belongs to me. Just to me. This is not surprising; I am well acquainted with the preservation process. It doesn't worry me. Not exactly. Not when each resurrection is different. Everybody knows each resurrection is different.

Still...

"Human cells die every day, you know."

The reassurance, unexpectedly given, is meant to stop my racing thoughts. Instead, it stops my racing heart. Though what speaks is not my sister, Its words are being woven with the loom of the dead girl's larynx. That is my sister's voice. Even if her lips are not yet in sync enough to provide the illusion of speech, *that is my sister's voice.*

"Millions of them," It continues in my sister's voice. "Hundreds of millions. At any given instant, you may be more dead than alive and not even realize it. This body, your body, all mortal bodies are... unintelligent. However, that is what makes them perfect Vessels. Because these automatous machines are already accustomed to shambling around in states of decay, I need but give this one a tiny push to make it move again."

My sister's body contorts into no less than four distinct shapes as she makes her explanations. When finished, her left arm looks strung up by fishhooks, and her right dislocated, while hands that have never been as delicate as mine twitch on their ends. There is a grotesque elegance to the way that her vertebrae grate against one another when she bends further, further, further, back, back, back into an arc that is still somehow less dramatic than the curve of her grin.

I count all twenty-eight teeth in her inverted smile. Better that than try to process my emotions.

"So you... You don't need my help?" I ask, if only to say something. To *do* something. I don't want to *think* yet. "You don't need me to—to help you walk out of the Catacombs, or...?"

"I need no more than what you have already given."

Wide eyes catch my own, irises bleached two shades from white by what shines within the cavity that once contained a soul. Whatever this entity is—god or devil, monster or spirit—It is mine now.

Mine for now.

Mine to take home.

It is tradition to name one's "new companion" after the gift they promised. I'm not sure why. Maybe to serve as a reminder between mortal and divine. Maybe to spare the deities the shame of admitting they can no longer remember their old names. Or maybe it's just a roundabout way to brag.

It is nothing short of blasphemous to speak about pacts forged in the Catacombs. Doing so is forbidden.

Doing so *explicitly* is forbidden, anyway.

And so, I cannot *explicitly* say who keeps to this tradition. Some, I would imagine. Not everyone. A few, I've gathered, were quite studious in their commitment to the idea, while others have taken a laxer, or more creative, approach.

Whatever the breakdown, it is the reason our communal language is now colored by Japanese and by Latin, by Rotarin and French and Greek and Xhosa and Egyptian and English and Sarcee and Gralinni. Of the ten thousand books in the High Priestess's holy library, over half are dictionaries. It is to these that I am allowed access—just like those who came before me—when the corpse who was my sister and I call upon the High Priestess the morning after our successful return from the Catacombs.

In the kaleidoscopic light of orsi stained glass, my not-sister reads up on what history she has missed. I comb through endless tomes of names. To my frustration, knowing the kind of name that I'm looking for does not make the task less challenging. If anything, it makes it more so.

But I am the one whose fingers can create delicate work. Delicacy cannot be attained without patience, and patience breeds its own sort of tenacity. Eventually, I find it, straightening from my slouch against the cool adobe wall.

"Izso," I announce.

The former idol glances up, equal parts stained and haloed by prismatic mandalas. "Hmm?"

"That's the name I've chosen for you," I explain. "Izso. It's... Hebrew, according to this book. Which was a language, I guess."

She nods, slow. Contemplative. Nostalgic. "It was."

"Well. All right, then. That's. That's decided," I say, clearing my throat. "Izso is what you will be called."

"Indeed? Hmmm. 'Izso'..."

The deity who has housed Itself within my sister's corpse repeats Its new name, again and again, in low tones and high tones and completely tonelessly. It hasn't been long, but she has already gained impressive control over her lip movements.

Other fine motor skills are also being honed. Izso demonstrated as much by methodically plucking the halo of petals from the celebratory pimpernel crown that the High Priestess's brother dropped upon her head when she'd crossed the threshold into the house. Now she is ringed by a mobius chain of unsanctified heads, and frankly seems happier for it.

"Very well," she decrees after a time. "*Izso* I shall be. Why not? In the end, it matters little how humanity refers to me, for names are so often lost, forgotten, or misremembered, anyway. And I shall be what I am regardless of any attached title.

"But what about *you*, my unsullied victor?"

A fair question. What *about* me? Glancing askance, I run a finger along my book's spine, feeling when I do something shiver down my own.

Quietly, I tell her, "I also... am what I am."

Izso's smile reminds me of the Catacombs, dark and long and full of stolen bones.

"*Oh ho*," she chuckles. "And you are...?"

⋯⊰◈⊱⋯

I am in training, like the other young people in our village.

Traditionally, this means studying theology under aunts. Weaponry with mothers. Uncles teach their nieces and nephews about histories, literatures, and cultures other than our own, while grandmothers and grandfathers instruct on the practical matters, like beadwork and protective magics and navigation and technology.

But I am apprenticed to our—to *my*—father. Some would argue that mine is the most important and sacrosanct training of all.

"An *undertaker*. I should have guessed." Izso giggles, her waxen hand melting down the warm sides of embalming bottles. Needles shine in a line on the table beside her, mercurial, providing a warped reflection of her amusement.

I tweak my expression with the same delicacy for which Father praises me. The same delicacy I would a cadaver's. "Why? Because your Vessel is so magnificently preserved?"

"Because no one else would have seen the great value of my offer."

She examines the frame of my newest cremation coffin, pushing nails into carved boards. Someday soon, I'll train Izso to assist with those tasks that hands like hers can do, much as Father's companion helps him: by bunching asphodel and dodecatheon, by buying relevant chemicals, by talking to the bereaved. For now, though, I allow her to prowl and slink and sniff and settle into the parlor, if only because it keeps her entertained while I carve a liturgy of funerary runes into the coffin's lid.

It is easier to talk to her when I don't have to look at her. Over time, I hope this will change. I assume it will change.

But then, I'd also assumed I would die first.

My sigh scatters wooden curls and juniper perfume across the parlor's backroom.

"...*Blood and promise bind us, you and I*," I recite. The words resonate differently here than they had in the Catacombs. "*When my blood runs dry and your promise is realized...*"

"...*nevermore shall we rise*," Izso finishes. "I remember. It was but days ago we made that pact, silly."

"And you meant it."

It is not a question, so it makes sense that Izso does not answer.

"It's just," I mutter, "I have handled so many dead bodies. Human, Vessel. There are some I feel intensely for, and some, nothing at all. We're not entirely different, in that respect. You have seen death, too. The loss of your people, the expiry of your religion. I don't doubt it was a traumatic experience. But so far, despite the depths of our emotions, our only losses have been… *external*.

"True death, when it comes for us, will be intimate. It will be more *final* than any battle, more *permanent* than any abandonment. My understanding of matters like philosophy and theology might be *lacking*, but I have seen enough of nature to know that it is forever-striving towards equilibrium. The days are half-light, half-dark. The years are half-cold, half-hot. There are deserts *and* oceans. Plains *and* mountains. Babies are born and the elderly pass. Human death precedes a chosen god's new life, and so what of every blessing given?

"It seems… To me, it seems a curse must follow."

These grim thoughts betray far more than my profession: they reveal the tarnished cogs of me, the creaking inner workings that have been grinding ceaselessly since the day that I first learned about the haunted, omnist cemetery that is the Catacombs.

I startle when I notice just how close Izso has crept. There is a softness to her now—to her gaze, to her voice, to her step—that I can only describe as *uncanny*.

"What are you proposing, precisely, little one?" she prompts. "That our heavenly gifts become the tortures of hell once our time here is up?"

Pale eyes ascend like twin stars above the horizon of the coffin lid, a pair of contrasting Polaris lights. I feel the urge to follow but cannot tell the way.

Instead, I look down at the woodgrain, at its bleak, mazelike patterns. I trace one of its trails, and know that I am approaching the borders of a different sort of blasphemy. I am skirting its edges as I would the hinge-work of a coffin.

But then, these are the sorts of things I have always prayed about. Why not discuss them with a god?

"I... Maybe."

"*Maybe?*"

"In the ancient societies," I tell her, "rulers tried to dictate morality by promising their followers posthumous rewards. Riches and virgins and happiness in an afterlife. But then, those ancient societies were not as entwined with the divine as we are. So... maybe we, in this modern age, are being paid in advance. Maybe our judgement comes early, while standing amongst the dead rather than lying with them. Maybe we're pulling angels from above, only to fashion them into our own personal demons."

The corners of Izso's mouth rise. They curve into a crescent moon, silvery and mirror-smooth, and I can see my own face in the bone structure of my dead sister's features.

I find myself thinking of the damned, of the delivered. Of how badly I wanted to die first.

Izso hums again, a habit that is fully her own.

"In some of those more ancient societies," she patiently purrs, "ignorance was said to have been called 'bliss.' If this was really your one chance at paradise, child, wouldn't it have been wiser to ignore the truth?"

"If companionship was your one chance to escape the Cat-acombs," I counter, "wouldn't it have been wiser to offer my predecessors something tangible and shallow?"

"…touché."

My ears blister beneath the heat of Izso's preternatural gaze. There is an emotion pulsing behind those eyes, and it is visceral, cosmic and terrible. It is beautiful and exultant and eternal. It is a sentiment that defies definition, much like this entity Itself, but just as convention had compelled me to name Izso, so too does human nature compel me to name this.

I will give you nothing, the effigy had vowed.

If everything really *does* balance back to zero, that might be the only salvation available to someone like me.

We pass a minute in silence.

"You know," Izso then says, conversational. "While you sought my newest name, I skimmed a story from a civilization that came after my own. It bored me, a bit. Perhaps something lost in translation, or to time. But in that story, there was a character with *your* name. A man who, like you, understood death and divinity more intimately than his peers. And to that man, it was said there was nothing he and his brother could not do, no joy they could not face, no doubt they could not kill, no height to which they could not ascend, so long as they did it together. So long as they kept their hands entwined."

I can still feel Izso staring, tender with veneration. There is to that stare the delicacy my sister lacked, and I know in the core of my bones that Izso could carve epitaphs into my sanity with the same elegance I could a grave marker.

"From the blinding dark to the blinding light," she admires, reverential. "I shall worship you all of our days, Enkidu."

Visceral, cosmic and terrible; beautiful and exultant and eternal. I shudder, because mankind struggles to withstand its own love. There will be no surviving the love of a god.

But then, I suppose, death itself was never the question.

"And I shall worship you, Izso."

Setting down my chisel, I brush the lid of the coffin clean. Motes of dust swirl about the workshop, vanishing into nihility as I take a moment to admire this once-mighty thing. By my power, it is limbless and bare, reduced to golden coils and broken rings: a lifeless vessel for a doomed soul and an empty husk.

With my hand gently, unseeingly extended, I say to my companion:

"Come. This is ready to be burned."

Major Key Inspiration:
The Epic of Gilgamesh

Quick Favor

Thank you so much for dedicating your time to reading this book! May we ask a quick favor?

Will you please take a moment to leave a review on Amazon, Goodreads, or wherever you purchased the book? Your words have power. Your review can help this book reach more readers. We appreciate you!

About M. Regan

M. Regan has been writing for over two decades, with credits ranging from localization work to short stories, poetry to podcast scripts. Fascinated by the fears personified by monsters, they enjoy dark fiction, studying supernatural creatures, and traveling to places rich with folklore. Pick up a copy of their soulful debut novella, 21 GRAMS wherever you buy your books or on Timber Ghost Press's website. Connnect with them on Twitter (@MReganFiction), Facebook (mreganfiction), and inside fairy rings (on special occasions).

acknowledgements

"Deep" was first published in *Shadows at the Door: An Anthology* by Shadows at the Door Publishing.

"Holy Water" was first published in the podcast *The Wicked Library: 2021 Pride Month Horror Special*.

"Sparrow" was first published in *Haunted House Short Stories* by Flame Tree Publishing.

"Gnothi Seauton Audio Tour" was first published in *Shadows at the Door: The Podcast* by Shadows at the Door Publishing.

"FPS<tag>" was first published in *Because That's Where Your Heart Is* by Sans. PRESS.

"The Magpie" was first published in *Women of the Woods* by Fabled Collective.

"Siren Song" is original to this collection.

"Corpse Road" is original to this collection.

"Unfair Grounds" is original to this collection.

"Umibozu" was first published in *Pirate & Ghost Short Stories* by Flame Tree Publishing.

"Fæge," under the title "Prescience," was first published in *Connections: The Podcast* by We Talk of Dreams.

"Catacombs" was first published in the podcast *Thirteen* by Imaginary Comma.

More great titles from Sobelo Books
available at www.SobeloBooks.com
and wherever books are sold.